Campbell Helling

To my family. I don't think I
could do this without you, and a
big thank you to Ms. Barbour,
who guided me every step of the
way.

                C.E.H

Chapter 1- Sparkle

Ten years ago-

I woke up from the interesting dream I had been having. The long, dark hall creaked under my three-year-old footsteps.

I opened the door to my mom and dad's bathroom, the bathroom with two sinks and the blue toilet. Something caught my eye.

It was glittery and amazing and I had to see it! The tile was cold as I walked to my mother's sink. On top of it, beautiful glimmering jewelry. I took hold of all of it, thinking it was the plastic play stuff at the dollar store.

I then had an idea. An idea that was magnificent in my mind, yet it was terrible in reality.

When the light cast upon the window above the toilet was shining just right, thousands of dollars slid right out of my small palm into the toilet, and I let it sparkle as I danced around the bathroom.

Ten years later-

I strolled down the carpeted stairs of my new foster house, Ms. Grande. The stairs led down to the kitchen, but I passed across, ignoring the smell of milk and cereal. I then walked into the living room, with two chairs, a sofa, and TV. The place that appealed to me most was the old, greasy chair in front of the TV. I turned the television set on, not paying any attention to it. I had other things to think about, like the fact I had criminal parents. Yes, they rob jewelry stores. Because of me, I may add.

Ms. Grande had sparkling yet curious blue eyes, grayish hair that was obviously attempted to be dyed brown, and a big mouth. The first thing she asked us when we got to her small house on Yeti Road was, "Now, little darlings, what do your parents steal?" I think she was just making sure they didn't rob houses, like some of our other cautious foster parents.

The foster parents before Ms. Grande were Mrs. and Mr. Malcolm. By far they are my favorite "parents." Poppy, my sister and I felt right at home when the green door opened for us. Unfortunately, Mrs. Malcolm was going to have babies, so they kicked us out to make room for twins. Apparently they did not want me or Poppy around because we were "too much trouble," and they also "didn't have enough room in their house" even though their house is spacious compared to other foster homes.

The news on the TV flashed before me, and I started to smile when I saw the headline: Police shortage, hiring sixteen-year-olds. The news man went on that criminals were revolting in jails, making more and more police quit. This was my chance to prove myself. I could catch my parents, and we could be a family again.

Although I am not sixteen, I am almost 6ft tall and mature when I have to be. I have been called fifteen before in the past. Would I take for sixteen? I was only thirteen.

"Hello. My name is Reagan Green. I am sixteen years old and I am interested in becoming a police officer," I said to the voice on the other end of the line.

"Please hold." Because of criminals are having their own revolts, they hire on the spot. No training, and simpler missions. I was praying I would get assigned my parent's case, but with my luck, that will never happen. Part of me also felt that if I did, something bad would happen.

The police department needed parents/guardians to sign a contract saying that they will allow me to go through with the process and risk my life etc. etc. Mom and dad certainly would flip if I asked them to sign my contract. I almost laughed at the thought.

Getting Ms. Grande to sign my contract was very easy. She had a bat's eyesight, and she didn't really pay attention to Poppy, my sister and I. The contract the police would send me by mail wouldn't arrive until a few more days, so I decided to let Poppy know of my plan.

Knock knock. "Come in." My sister was sitting on her bed, daydreaming. Since she had known about mom and dad, she had been acting distant, but obedient. Ms. Grande discovered that, so she worked poor Poppy like her own personal servant. Poppy had a mile long list of chores, while I had none, and I had offered multiple times to do them. Poppy continuously said no, to let her do the work, so I let her do everyone on the list, although I feel like it is wrong and something that I should stop.

"Hey, Poppy how would you feel if I caught mom and dad so we could be a family?"

"Are you going to?" for the first time in months her voice sounded interested.

"I think that I am."

Chapter 2 - Police Station

Ten years ago-

I had been admiring the scene when my mom walked into the bathroom. I knew I was in trouble, so I quickly flushed the toilet. I tried to tip-toe out, but mom saw me.

It was over, I realized.

"Sweetie, have you seen mommy's jewels?" I couldn't reply. Tears rolled down my plump, rosy cheeks and then mom asked, "Reagan, where are they?" The tears started to downpour, and I could tell mom was getting annoyed and angry.

"Reagan Lucille, where is the jewelry?" Ashamed, I pointed to the toilet.

Mom grabbed my arm and marched me to my dad, who was reading yesterday's newspaper.

"Guess what your eldest daughter just did," She said in a snarky, annoyed voice.

"I don't know, hon. What did she do?" Dad asked, eying me in the way he always did when he was about to get mad at me.

"She flushed all of my jewelry down the toilet!"

"Reagan Lucille Green! You do not flush anything down the toilet unless it came out of you! You are grounded miss."

I staggered to my room. When I got in my room, I had felt worse than I did ever before. My straight, blonde hair was in tangles and my clear, brown eyes were now cloudy and red. Tears streamed down my face, one by one.

Ten years later-

Ms. Grande dropped me off at the police station a few days after I got her to sign my contract. I just told her the contract was for extra homework.

Ms. Grande thought that the police station was hosting a dog training learning event. I informed her that, and so she believed me. I felt bad lying, but couldn't tell her the lie. I had to later, after I got assigned a mission, so it would have been done.

"Have fun Reagan," Ms. Grande said. "Tell me about the dogs when I pick you up!"

"Bye," and I trudged up to the brick building.

There was a whoosh of warm air when opened the glass door to the station, and the linoleum floor clicked as I walked on it.

"Hello," a voice said. "You must be Sadie?" The voice was the receptionist, who had frizzy black hair and huge glasses.

"Actually, I am Reagan," I replied.

"Are you here for the job? Go down the hall and turn right and there will be a door. Go through it and ask for Lydia," the receptionist said, almost like she rehearsed it for a play.

"Thanks."

I went down the hallway, took a right and opened the door that the receptionist said there would be. Inside there was a group of people, all looked around sixteen.

"I-Is anyone n-named L-L-Lydia?" I stammered.

A woman who looked much older than sixteen raised her hand. She had curly brown hair, and a calm, inviting voice.

"I'm Lydia," she smiled. Lydia held out her hand, and I shook it.

"I am Reagan Green." She laughed.

"I know, sweetheart. Come with me, and I will give you a rundown on your mission, and I will introduce your partner in crime to you."

I laughed at her joke.

We strolled down to a door that led to outside, or so I thought.

"Since our only time outside is fighting crime, we like to 'look outside' by pasting images of the great outdoors on doors and windows," Lydia explained. I smiled as we walked down yet another hallway.

"Your partner's name is Nillian, but she goes by Nilly. She is sixteen, and this also is her first mission," Lydia said. She got out a silver key with a green ribbon on it, and opened a door with the numbers 48 painted on the dark oak wood.

"Although regular police don't sleep in dorms, you guys will since normal police have family to take care of. You will visit your family on weekends and holidays, so don't worry. You should not be homesick, but call for me if you are."

It took a lot to take in what Lydia just said. Poor Poppy was stuck with Ms. Grande until I came back to them.

Chapter 3 - Nilly Zarccoo

Inside the dorm, there was two twin sized beds, a closet and a desk. On one of the beds sat a girl with a brown pixie cut, freckles, and a purple shirt.

"I'm Nilly," she introduced herself.

"My name is Reagan." She smiled, and motioned for me to sit down next to her.

"Can I call you Regs?" she asked, clearly trying to be my friend.

"Um...sure? I don't know."

"Anyway, what school do you go to?"

Oh no. Sixteen year olds go to high school. I'm in eighth grade. Should I say I'm homeschooled or...

"I go to Shakespeare High," I blurted. Shakespeare High was one of the two high schools in our town. The other high school was Smithton High.

"Cool. I do to. What grade are you in?"

"Sophomore. I'm a sophomore." I barely managed to conceal my lie.

"I am the grade after that," Nilly laughed.

Since I didn't bring anything to the police station such as clothing and toothbrushes because I had no clue we needed them, I had to call Ms. Grande. It was time to tell her the truth. I dialed her number on Lydia's cellphone, since I didn't have one. The number felt long as I pressed against the screen. I could already feel Ms. Grande's anger.

"Hello Ms. Grande, I was wondering if you could possibly bring down clothing and my bathroom necessities. I am sorry, but I just signed up to be a police officer to do good and well, catch my parents," I explained.

"You lied?!"

"Yes. I'm sorry, but this is my chance to catch my parents, who are still out there doing bad stuff. I want to catch them so we can be a true family. Again," I admitted.

"Darling, it is not that simple-"

"I know. Mom and dad will be locked up behind bars for a while. Then we can be together. I miss them."

"What about your safety?"

"I will be fine. They won't assign me dangerous missions. Just...challenging."

"And you have to be twelve?" Ms. Grande asked.

"Something like that." And then I hung up.

That night I met Nilly when we (as in all the rest of the 16+ police) traveled next door to Sandra's Cooking, an Italian restaurant. Inside was a buffet, so we all got takeout after selecting our third course.

Nilly and I ate and talked about "high school life." All I really did was listen, but what they say is true. Lying does get easier the more you do it. Nilly sees me as a sophomore, who's homeroom teacher is Mr. D'Angelo, and apparently Ms. Grande is my math teacher. How coincidental.

Chapter 4 – The Assignment

Ten years ago-

I sat in my room waiting for my mom to tell me everything was okay, and it was just a dream. Just a bad dream. But I heard the door open and close, and the words "jewelry store" and "make up for it." Fearful, I crept down the staircase to my parent's room. Their door was closed, yet I still opened it.

Just a crack.

Inside, my parents were packing hammers and masks into backpacks.

"They must be doing a project," I whispered to myself. A project was for adults only, so I didn't know exactly what they did. All I knew was it sometimes involved bad words.

"Doing a project," sneered a nasty, frightful voice. My little heart pounded as I close my eyes. A hand grasped my shoulder, so I opened them. In front of me was my dad. His eyes were blood-red, and he was steaming.

The door was wide open now, and I could see that mom and dad were not packing hammers, masks and guns for a "project." No. They were doing something else. Even though I was stupid enough to flush diamonds down the toilet, I recognized that what they were doing was immoral. And scary.

I ran up the stairs, down the hall that led to my room. I closed my door, locked it, and found one-year-old Poppy sitting on my bed, drinking her orange-juice. I staggered over to her, my tears falling for the third time today. I wrapped my shaking arms around her as she patted my back, knowing that I was scared and sad all at the same time.

Ten years later-

The next morning we were assigned missions. "Peter Brooks and Georgia Perinial, you have the Julius Cano case," the police chief, Chief Walters read off of a list. Nilly and I were last on the list, since Nilly's last name was Zarccoo. "Nilly Zarccoo and Reagan Green, you are on the Nick and Dawna Green case."

My head began to spin. I thought I wanted this mission, but I realized that I wasn't ready for this. I never was. Over and over my whole life flashed back and forth. From my second birthday to my thirteenth year on this planet. I sat down, but it was no use.

I could only see black after that.

I awoke to the sound of voices. My delicate eyelids opened, and light flooded in like the river during a rainy season. My head hurt. No, it throbbed, without sign of stopping.

I sat up, in a strange room. There was a couch, chairs and a rug. That was it. Everything was some sort of purplish color.

"W-Where a-a-am I?" My jaw hurt, and it was a miracle that I could talk. Then I heard Lydia's voice.

"You're in the women's lounge, hon. That was a nasty fall. Can I get you a Tylenol? The only sound I could get out of my tender mouth was a groan.

Later that evening, I sat in my dorm with Nilly.

"So what did you freak out when we were assigned that case?" Nilly asked, showing pure curiosity.

"They were just family friends. They have two daughters," I stammered. My head still hurt, and lying to Nilly didn't help the pain.

"Cool. It's funny how you have the same last names," She remarked as she eyed the file Chief Walters gave to us.

"It really is," I muttered, almost too quiet to hear.

Chapter 5 - Sixteen

My list of fears

Becoming like mom and dad

Poppy getting hurt

Mom and dad will find out that I'm on their track.

Nilly will find out my lies

???

I wrote these words down on a sheet of paper as an activity for my "Jr. Team Group." Mine consisted of Lydia, who was the leader, Margaret, an eighteen-year-old, Nilly, and Suzanne, who looked oddly familiar.

The rest of the police decided that the younger department should be split up into teams to help us with our assignment, because we got no training except how to fire a gun when needed.

There are around fifteen teams. We do daily activities, and this activity was to privately write down our fears and if we wanted to, we could share them with our team. I was certainly not going to. I suspected Nilly thought I was related with our criminals, which I was. I was their daughter!

After the meeting, it was bedtime. I combed my long, blonde hair and brushed my teeth. Nilly just looked at me. "Are you sure you are sixteen? You look much younger."

"I um, was a premature baby. I was small my whole life." Nilly almost seemed to scan me; she looked up and down and up and…

"Very small." And she burst out laughing.

"Okay, my height isn't very small, perhaps but the rest of m-"

"I was just kidding. You look fine, in fact maybe older than sixteen." I only smiled, thankful that I looked "older than sixteen."

Although I fell asleep late that night, I woke up early, admiring my first good dreams in a while. I dreamt of me with my parents and Poppy. We were all laughing at my dad's jokes, and everything in the past was forgotten and nonexistent.

We were a family again, in my dream.

Chapter 6 - Necklace

Ten years ago-

Poppy and I held together for a while, until our parents' ugly voices were gone. We then looked at each other, and I did what any stupid three-year old would do: I walked to the bathroom with the blue toilet and dipped my hand in, then slowly but surely my hand went deeper, and deeper until it touched the bottom of the toilet.

Yes. I was trying to retrieve the jewelry.

I heard the front door open. I quickly forced my arm out of the toilet bowl and wiped it on my mother's robe, which she got when she went to Spain when she was in college. I ran out of the bathroom, up the stairs and into the bedroom, where Poppy was still sitting. I closed the door, locked it and dove under the pink, horse covers mom had got me for my second birthday.

I was breathing hard when someone knocked on the door. "Who there?" Poppy asked, as she unlocked the door. I heard footsteps, and Poppy squeal excitedly. "A necklace!" I popped my head out of the blankets and looked in the direction of the

door. In the doorway stood my mother and father in a good mood.

Poppy and I admired our new necklaces as mom and dad went to "unpack." Mine was a butterfly, with pink diamonds and it was gold plated. Poppy's was the same, except her diamonds were purple.

We both went downstairs to ask mom to help us put the necklace on, but we both stopped in front of the closed door that led to the dining room. Our parents were whispering, yet we could still hear them.

"What about the police? Do you think they will find out?" A voice that sounded familiar to my mother inquired.

"We both have good reputations. No one will suspect one bit."

"Well, Nick, anyone to the police is a suspect."

"Calm down. A few more runs and you will have what your jewelry is worth back."

"Nick, it's not how I want to live."

"Dawna, calm down. Like I said before, only a few more runs."

"Okay. I trust you."

Poppy and I crept away from the door, unsure what we had just witnessed. Together, we climbed the stairs to my bedroom. We both laid down on my twin bed to take a nap, with our necklaces still clutched in our hands.

Chapter 7 – Dawna and Nick Green

It was day one of our mission. First, we strolled together to the filing room. The door creaked open, and inside were cabinets and cabinets of files! It was a maze to find

the "G" section. Once we did, it took about half an hour to find the right Green case.

"Grow, Groow, Groz, I can't find Green." Nilly remarked

"Go back a few files."

"Green, Amanda, Green, Alex, Green, Allie, Green, Andrew, Green, Annie"

"Go forward a bit more."

"Green, Naomi, Green, Nate and Barry, Green, Nathan, and Green, Nick and Dawna"

"That is it!" I said, enthusiastically.

Nilly pulled the manila file out of its place, and set it down on a table nearby. We opened it up, and right away an old, crumpled picture of their wedding day fell out. The picture I had looked at so many times, falling in love with my mother's white dress, and my father's handsome smile.

"You kind of look like her," Nilly said, noting the similarity between my mother and I.

"Let's look at the documents," I said, trying to change the subject.

In the file were crisp, clear papers nobody had reviewed. I knew this because it was obvious; no stains, no wrinkles, no pencil marks.

"Let us get cracking!"

For hours Nilly and I stayed in the filing room, reviewing my parent's papers.

"Spotted at Bling Bling Jewelry Store about a month ago, stole rings and necklaces," I muttered to Nilly, who was also reviewing their most recent robbery.

"It's funny they steal only jewelry. I wonder why," Nilly said

"Yeah. It really is." And I went back to reviewing the papers.

Chapter 8 - Fourth Birthday

Staying up until midnight was worth finding out all the information about my parents. We found out they have robbed up to 30 jewelry stores, and they usually rob in this city. I already knew that, but I pretended I didn't.

The truth is, since they put me in foster care when I was seven, I have been researching my parent's case. Some nights I only got two hours of sleep. But no one knows that. Not even Poppy, who I told about mom and dad only about a month ago. This was one of my many secrets.

One of many secrets.

"Hey, Reagan, do you want to celebrate our research with some candy tonight?" Nilly asked me.

"Sure." I shrugged as we were walking Sandra's Cooking for breakfast. I had never been to a party before. I don't have any friends. I remember my first friend out of two almost nine years ago...

It was my fourth birthday, so I was in an especially good mood. I was wearing my gold butterfly necklace, and my favorite pink dress. December was always my favorite month, but having it be my birthday month was even better. I had always thought of 6 as a fond number, but it being my birth date was the best. Yep, I rocked December 6 like it was my favorite dress.

The only bad thing about my 4th birthday: it was on a daycare day. And so December 6 was the day I threw an award-winning tantrum. I'm not kidding. I could have won an Oscar.

"I don't want to go to daycare," I said, trying to sound as miserable as I could.

"Darling. We have been over this. Yes, you have to go to daycare. Mommy and daddy have work to do, so you have no choice."

I grumped my way to the kitchen, where my winter coat and boots were, and thrust the coat on my shoulders. "Now put on the boots," My mother said, who was now standing front of me.

"No," I refused.

"Reagan, we don't have time for this."

"Yes we do," I sassed back.

"Reagan, if I say your name one more time..."

"Say it. Say it loud and I still won't go to daycare."

"Reagan Lucille Green! Put on your boots, and no birthday gifts will be taken away."

"Everyone loves me! If you take away a gift, I'll get another one."

"One present goes away in 3..."

"No!"

"2..."

"I will get more!"

"1 ½ ..."

"I can't hear you! Banana nana banana nana banana nana!"

"1."

I screeched like a parrot, and mom picked me up, marched to the garage, then opened the car door and forced me into my car seat. She started the old, rusty engine to our old Chevy, and backed out of our driveway.

When we arrived at my daycare, I was still throwing my fit. My mom walked with me to the check-in, and took me to the four-year-old room.

After she left, I started crying in the coloring corner. It was very hard to concentrate on coloring my "Princess Petunia" coloring book. As I was coloring Petunia's hair, a girl went up to me. "Hi I'm Rosie and I love unicorns and mermaids and I really really really don't like pirates," she said. I smiled, wiped the tear that was falling from my eye, and stood up. "Me too," I said. We started holding hands, and dashed off to the furry friend land. We played with Timmy the turtle, Gary the giraffe, and Harris the hedgehog. They all battled pirates (and won), turned into mermaids, and they rode on a unicorn to a rainbow. By the time my mother picked me up, we both had forgotten about my "little" tantrum, and were in good moods.

"I met a friend. Now she is my best friend and her name is Rosie!" Mom laughed, and said, "Do you want to see my new earrings when we get home?"

"Yes!"

```
Chapter 9- 364 Newfound Rd.
```

Rosie eventually moved away around a year or two later. I think it was somewhere in Alaska. Our moms were good friends, and they arranged Rosie to visit in 1st grade. She hung around for about a week, and in that time she befriended a girl. The girl that would later bully me in 6th grade. The only thing that stopped her from her bullying was moving to North Dakota, which is far away from this little town in Colorado called Smithton.

Nilly and I spent the rest of the day in the filing room, going through my parent's case. We found almost nothing, since no one has ever investigated it.

"I think it is time to go out and find these people." I looked up at Nilly, and only could blink.

"Do you think we are prepared?"

"Yeah. We have all the info we need."

"Are you sure?"

"Yep. 101% sure," Nilly said.

I took a deep breath and said, "We are ready."

"Anyway, are you ready to party?"

I winked at Nilly and said, "Ready as I'll ever be."

And I was. For nine years, I have had no friends but two; I was that kid who ate alone. That kid who didn't have a partner to partner up with in science class. That kid who sat on the swings, while everyone else played hide-and-seek. But now I was different. I had one friend.

And her name was Nilly Zarccoo.

Lydia waved goodbye as she gave us a map to the house, even though I didn't need it. Nilly and I pulled out of the parking lot in her small car. First stop, my old house.

"What is the address of their house again?" Nilly asked.

"364 Newfound Rd. Turn left onto Asbury Lane..." Nilly turned her blinker on, and turned into a tree covered road that looked familiar. Then all the sudden, a memory flashed before my eyes...

It was officially fall, Poppy's favorite season. A couple of streets down was her so-called "hideout." She called it that because on the street were many, many trees. But one was special. So special, it had a hole big enough for a young girl, plus her older sister to fit in. We would glance out to the ever-changing, decaying world we live in. We found peace just staring at the softly falling, autumn leaves and the cars passing by. It was wonderful. Just Poppy and I, alone in the vast world.

"Reagan. Focus. Now where do we turn?" Nilly asked, obviously annoyed.

"Sorry. Had a memory." Now the car was parked directly left of the "hideout."

"Where do I turn?"

"Turn right onto Mulberry Lane."

Nilly did, and then out of memory I said, "Now turn left and then another left. Drive down about 300 feet, and look to your right. You will see a dirt road, and that is the driveway. Drive down it another hundred or so feet, look in my direction and you will see a brick house. That is exactly 364 Newfound Rd." I opened my eyes, which I did not realize I closed.

The car jerked to a stop, and then I had grasped what I just told.

"Okay. Something is up. Tell me now. You just told me the rest of the way to that house, without glancing at the map. That is insane."

"They are just really good family friends. We used to joke with the Greens that we almost lived with them," I tried. I could tell Nilly didn't believe me, but she did not say anything.

I had to repeat my instructions to her- using the map. I didn't want her to think I was the offspring of the robbers we were catching, yet I was. I knew it wouldn't be long until she found out-I get a stinging, burning feeling inside.

I got that same feeling when the police came and took Poppy and I away from our parents so many years ago. I still remember Poppy screaming and crying as the police guided us to the white and black car with the sirens off. I walked with them, obedient and silent. Poor Poppy was terrified; she was always close to our mother. The police car drove away from the long, dirt driveway that led to our house.

Nilly halted to a stop just before the driveway. I could tell it was different. Instead of gray dirt that got the old Chevy dusty, there was cement. Glowing, white cement.

Nilly turned to me and asked, "Are you ready?"

I nodded, and we drove down to the long, familiar way to my house, the one I grew up in until I was seven. I closed my eyes and when we stopped, I slowly opened them.

Chapter 10- Changes

The once bright red brick house was now painted a dazzling white, like the driveway. The old, wooden antique front door was replaced with a modern white one, and the black shutters were painted an olive green. It was a new house. It wasn't warm and welcoming like when I used to live in it. It wasn't a home anymore.

It was a house.

We parked right in front of the new front door, as I straightened the shimmering gold badge on my navy blue polo shirt. Underneath it, an uncomfortable heavy bullet-proof vest. Lydia suggested putting it under our shirts for the first time, since people were skeptical about the sixteen-year-old-cops. That way they could see the official badge, and the embroidered police department logo on our right shoulder: Smithton Police Department.

"Are you ready to ask those questions?" It was me who asked Nilly, instead of her asking me.

"Yep."

The night before, me and Nilly found that my parents didn't reside in 364 Newfound Road anymore, so we stayed up until midnight coming up with questions for the new owners. Have you been robbed recently? Are you aware that the people who lived in your house before you were criminals? Do you have any knowledge of the whereabouts of them? How long ago did you move in? Did you notice anything unusual about the previous owners? Did you buy this house directly from them?

We tip-toed up to the door, and rang the doorbell. When I lived there, we didn't have a doorbell. Only a brass knocker in the shape of a whale. We called him Willy.

We heard multiple locks turn. Was this person paranoid and if so, about what? I counted seven locks opening when the door knob turned. It opened just a crack, and I noticed an icy blue eye, the same shade as my mother's eye.

"Who aww ya?" A woman's accented voice asked.

"This is Reagan and I'm Nilly. We are from the Smithton Police Department and we are here to discuss the case we are investigating with you. All you have to do is answer questions, and the whole process will be very short."

"Well, I suppose dat is all right. Cum on iyan."

The door opened very wide, and I gasped. All the furniture, all the pictures that were there when I lived in my house, they were all still there.

I looked over to the woman, and she was holding a bloody knife.

Chapter 11- Mother Dear

The knife was a regular kitchen knife, with an oak handle with metal engravings on it. I was standing a distance away, but I could still read it. March 25, 2009, was what was printed, and there were etches of faces. Then I realized whose faces they were: Poppy on the right side, my own features on the left.

I looked closely at the woman. She had reddish-brown hair in a ponytail, red lipstick and freckles. She wore a red T-shirt, white jeans, and to top it off, hot pink sneakers. Her look expressed a surprised character; she looked oddly familiar.

"Welcome home, Reagan Lucille. Long time no see," she spit out, pronouncing the "c" in Lucille long, to the point she sounded like a snake. Now the woman did not have the accent, and was speaking in a familiar voice that reminded me of someone I used to know very well, but who could it be?

"How do know my name?"

She chuckled, and replied, "It is simple dear, for I gave birth to you."

Now I understood it all. My parents painted the house and redid the driveway to make it look like someone new moved in. They pretended to buy it again.

"You were just too dumb, darling," mother mocked me, pacing in a circle around us. She was spinning the knife around like it was a toy.

I glanced around, looking for an escape path, but it was obvious none was available. The old maple floors creaked for every footstep my mother took. Nilly turned to me and gave me a look that read they are your parents? I nodded, ashamed of myself for telling Nilly all my lies.

A tear rolled down my cheek, and my cruel, cruel mother noticed. She smiled.

"Remember the time at the jewelry store? You did not suspect anything. Not one thing at all."

And I did remember. Exactly two weeks before my sister and I were taken away from my parents…

I didn't have school that day, so I slept in until 10:00am that morning. Waffles were waiting for me at the new breakfast table in the kitchen.

A few weeks earlier, we went to a furniture store nearby. My mom picked out a new table because our old one was "getting old," and it also had pen and paint stains since Poppy loved art. We called her Mini Picasso whenever she was drawing.

The sun shone through the car window, as we passed fields and fields of golden wheat. My parents didn't say where we were going, but I knew it was somewhere fun. They always took me to a place I would enjoy.

After 30 minutes of driving, we parked in a parking lot close by a jewelry store. Both parents put on ski masks.

"It might be cold out," stated my father, while handing me a pink and white mask even though it was spring "Make sure you keep it on, and don't ever take it off."

I giggled and willingly stretched the fabric around my head, and then I skipped to the store, holding hands with my parents.

When we got inside the jewelry store, my parents sat me down on one of the many chairs available and they told me to wait.

"Your mother and I have to go to the restroom," said my father who then rushed off with my mother. I kept myself occupied in the meantime by looking at a magazine one of the employees offered to me.

"Where are your parents, sweetie?" she asked me. Her name tag read Heather.

"They are going potty," I replied, giving Heather a toothless smile. "Mommy and daddy went back there." I pointed to the direction they went in, and Heather just shook her head slowly.

"Darling, I'm sorry but that area is restricted. Only people that work here can go in that door," she explained.

Just as she told that to me, a wailing alarm went off, and two people with black ski masks on ran out of the store, grabbed me, and put me in their car. I screamed and kicked and hollered for my life.

The two people took of the ski masks and I prepared to see pointy noses, warts, and grey hair but instead I was taken aback as I realized who they were. My parents. I only laughed, because that was what I did when I felt relieved.

We then played at a carnival, which I had spotted on the way to the jewelry store. I won a teddy bear at the ball and bucket toss.

By sunset I was snoring, and in dreamland. That night was probably the last night I had a good dream for years, and years, and years.

Chapter 12- Stab Wound

I will say, seeing your own mother holding a bloody knife, walking around you in circles, and not to mention threatening to kill you, can really change the way you think of the world.

"How is Poppy, Reagan darling?" My mother smiled mischievously.

I closed my eyes, praying my mother wouldn't harm Poppy; she is my one and only best friend, she is the only person I would die for. We have a very close bond, even though it doesn't appear that way. Before a year ago, she was a lighthearted, happy, joyful spirit. She even found beauty in a thunderstorm or blizzard.

Now, we almost didn't speak like we used to. Occasionally we share a round of laughter, but it was always fake. Never real. We both knew it was fake, yet we did not say what we thought ourselves.

"Poppy is fine." I made my answer short and sharp, so I wouldn't feed my mother any more information than she needed to know. Poppy shouldn't be in danger. For crying out loud our mother was holding a kitchen knife! And surprisingly, she was the very same mother who fed us, bathed us, put us to bed and much more so many years ago. We used to trust her. Used to trust her.

And now, she came closer to me, with the knife. Closer, closer. Every step to me she almost exaggerated. Each step was slower than the other one before. I closed my eyes, preparing to die. For Poppy. For Nilly. Even for Lydia and Ms. Grande.

"If you tell me where Poppy is living right now, I will not kill you. If you do not, your friend here will see you die." my mother was now next to me, whispering in my ear. I gulped.

"No."

My mother raised the knife with her right hand. That is unusual. I thought. She was left handed.

The knife unhurriedly came down. Sweat trickled down my face, as tears streamed and mixed with the other liquid on me.

"Good bye," my evil, rotten mother sneered to me. But I saw something in her. She was hesitant and afraid. Afraid to murder her eldest daughter. Afraid of the consequences she will face if she ever gets arrested.

"Before you kill her," Nilly started, "What is the date March 25, 2009, and what does it mean?" my mother turned around quickly, accidentally slicing me in the arm. I crumpled to the ground, wailing in agony. The misery and pain were almost too much to bear.

"Noth-thing. It m-means absolutely n-nothing," she stammered. Although I was in pain, I quickly searched my mind for the date on the knife. Then I remembered. The day my mother's own parents were killed in a car wreck on vacation in Florida.

The reddish brown hair spun back around to face towards me. Her once ice blue eyes were almost as if they were glowing a fiery red.

I whimpered, for my heart pounded faster and my wound was gushing blood faster, and faster. If my mother did not kill me with the knife, she could always lock me in a room and leave me to bleed to death. Of course I would never say that out loud, for I didn't want to give her any ideas.

Violently, mom heaved the knife towards me. It was sailing through the thin air, straight at my leg. I couldn't move. I was numb. I felt it gash into my thigh. Excruciating pain and misery blasted my leg like a bomb. The knife glared at me, and it taunted me as I howled as if I were a wolf.

I glanced at my mother, who was pale and frightened. Nilly was in just as much shock as my mother. She finally snapped out of her phase, and rushed over to my leg.

"Call 911," I murmured, because in my mind, speaking louder would only cause more torment to both my leg, and my arm, which was still streaming with blood.

Nilly fumbled with her phone, which she had in the back pocket of her navy blue slacks. She punched three numbers in it as fast as she could, and Nilly was fast.

"Hello? This is an emergency. I have a friend on 364 Newfound Road with two stab wounds. One on the arm, and the other is on her leg. The knife is stuck in the leg wound. And we also have Ms. Dawna Green with us." Pause. "Yes, the victim is conscious. Thank you." Pause. "The address is 364 Newfound Road." And then Nilly hung up.

When I glanced around for my mother, she was gone.

Not one trace of her.

Chapter 13 - March 25, 2009

Despite it being a Wednesday, Poppy and I didn't have school, therefore we were able to stay home. My mother was at the local gym while our babysitters, Isabella and Katrina sat for us. We were playing Candyland.

"My move!" Poppy declared.

"No! It's Katrina's turn. You went two times in a row last time, and nobody said anything," I complained.

"Thank you, Reagan. I appreciate you sticking up for me. And Poppy, if you want to take my turn just for this move you can," Katrina soothed.

I beamed at her, while Poppy joyfully made Katrina's yellow piece jump to the next orange space on the board.

"Hey girls, what do you want for lunch?" Isabella asked. And then the phone rang.

It was a phone call that changed my mother.

"Hello?" Isabella said, speaking into the phone sitting on the side table in the living area.

There was a pause, and then she spoke again.

"The police department?" another long pause.

"Mam, I'm sorry but I am only the babysitter. Mrs. Green is away right now."

She switched the phone to her other ear, as if she was making sure of what she was hearing.

"I'm sorry, can you please repeat what you just told me please?"

"Car wreck? Dead?" she murmured. When Katrina heard the word "dead" she swallowed hard.

"Yes, Mrs. Green's children are here with me." Another long and silent pause. She put her hand on the speaking part of the white phone and motioned for Poppy and I to come over. Slowly we did, expecting to hear about our mother's death.

Isabella handed me the phone. Hands shaking, I picked it up.

"Hello?" I gulped and shut my eyelids.

"This is the Smithton Police Department. Do you know Pierre and Lynn Cooke?"

"Yeah. They are my LaLa and Poppa. Why do you ask?"

"Sweetie, they were in a car wreck a few hours ago. They... they didn't make it. Honey, they died."

The woman's voice sounded sorry, yet I still took all my anger out on her.

"They were innocent! They didn't do anything! Were you the person that made LaLa and Poppa..."

And I then hung up the stupid, plastic phone by slamming it on its base and stomped up to my room.

Katrina brought up some warm tomato soup, yet it didn't appeal to me, nor did facing the idea of my very favorite grandparents dead.

Knock knock. Someone knocked on my bedroom door a few hours later. I was flipping through LaLa and Poppa's picture book they gave to me some time ago. There was them at their wedding-LaLa came from a very wealthy family. She and Poppa only had one daughter, which was my mother. I turned to the next page, which was them smiling holding a kitten. The caption below the yellowing picture read, "We got a new kitten! We named her Phyllis after Pierre's sister!" I sighed.

I got up and tiptoed to the door and turned the glimmering silver knob, slowly. I cracked the door open just a little and peeped through it. Outside standing directly in front of it was my crying sister.

"Mommy just is mad. And I don't know why," She cried, exaggerating "mad" and "why" long and with a groan.

I hugged her, and her tight shoulders loosened. We ignored my mother's anger by playing with her dolls in her room. We were at the part where the sister doll and brother doll were fighting over nonsense when our father called us for dinner. We took a deep breath and staggered down the never ending staircase.

Chapter 14 - Like a Ghost

Nilly stayed with me until the ambulance and police arrived. Once they did, Nilly drove away in her car, not looking back while the paramedics put me on an uncomfortable stretcher that smelled like disinfectant.

"Don't worry, darling. Everything is going to be fine. Your arm will be alright, although your leg might need some work on," A paramedic reassured me in a deep southern accent.

"Can you get the knife out of my leg right now? It is painful and it hurts," I complained. "If we removed the knife, it would be a heck a lot more painful and to top it all off, you could die of blood loss because it if blocking all of the blood vessels. Looking at it, I would expect it is lodged in your bone."

I gulped, and closed my eyes as they lifted me into the horrifying, yet the helpful ambulance that carried me all the way to the hospital.

The paramedics put a mask over my nose and mouth and pumped a chemical through the tube that led to a metal box. The gas made me very sleepy, so I was thinking it was laughing gas. Just before I fell into a deep, dark sleep, I noticed just at the corner of my eye a paramedic, who motioned at me, but when I turned my head, he was gone.

Like a ghost.

Finally, I woke up and when I did, I was in a different room with a strange bed, two plastic chairs and an old television. The old pastel yellow walls made my head spin. The bed I had slept in was different than any other I had seen before, but I do remember seeing one like it. When Poppy was born, I went to go visit my mother. I remember cuddling with her and kissing Poppy, who we thought we would name Susan. That was my first memory.

A woman in blue scrubs strolled in.

"Hello I am Isabella and I will be you nurse. You are Reagan, aren't you?"

"Yes." My voice almost cracked, but Isabella just laughed.

"I heard you got two stab wounds. Dr. Gummy will be with you soon, and he will tell you what he is going to do so he can remove the knife out of your femur."

I must've looked confused, so she explained for me what a femur is and also what they did to me while I was sleeping.

"All we did was we took X-rays of your right leg, and we discovered that the knife was very deeply imbedded in your bone. Unfortunately, we will have to surgically remove it and you will 'get' to stay with us for a few days. In the meantime, we will contact your parent or guardian to tell them what happened."

All I did was fall back to sleep.

Dr. Gummy slowly woke me up by snapping his fingers and by cutting off the gas I was inhaling.

"Hello, Ms. Reagan. How is your leg?"

I groaned and in misery I said, "It hurts like heck."

"I understand that. Can you tell me how you got this wound?"

"I am a police officer, and I had caught one of the two criminals I was assigned. She was armed with a knife, and she sliced my arm and she flung the knife into my leg. The end."

"Oh. Very...interesting," Dr. Gummy stated as if he didn't believe the story. "Now let me tell you what I will do to your leg."

He then went on and explained the whole process, which I didn't listen to. I only heard the bitter words "replace" and "cut." By the time he was done talking about all my leg, he called in two nurses to assist him during the operation. Isabelle and another nurse who introduced herself as Josephine. They rolled in a tray of sharp, metallic tools. Yet another mask went over my face as they rubbed green gel around the wound. I fell asleep for the third time that day, and again I saw the paramedic who disappeared when I looked at him, but this time I was too weak and exhausted to turn my head. I then closed my eyes, and went into a beautiful sleep.

Chapter 15 – Apology

One week later-

The woods were endless and unforgiving. We had been walking for miles looking for them. Finally, we came up to a shallow stream that was burbling a song. We laid down our heavy backpacks and took small sips of the sweet tasting water. It was almost too sweet for me, and when I turned around a ginormous grizzly bear was standing over us, as it almost seemed to say to us, "You know you are dead, right?"

I started into a sprint, running towards the snow-covered mountain. I looked back, and the bear was harassing Nilly.

"No!" I cried, but it was too late.

By the time I came back, Nilly was gone.

And in her place was a fresh pile of human bones.

Now-

My eyes flickered as I gently eased myself into being awake. There was a white cast on my whole leg, and when I tried to move it, it really hurt.

"Ow," I cringed. My mouth was hard to move, probably since I haven't been drinking any water. There were tubes and wires leading to my legs, arms, and even fingers. Then a voice startled me.

"Hello, Reagan. You are quite a sleeper," said a new nurse.

I meant to say "How long did I sleep for?" But the words came out as if I were speaking gibberish. "Ha one ih I eep?" I asked the kind nurse.

"You slept for about two days. You also made it through the worst of the pain you will be experiencing."

"Oo er you?" Or, "Who are you?" I asked her.

"Oh, you are right! I forgot to introduce myself to you. My name is Caroline. Isabella had an emergency so I am subbing for her."

"Ice," I replied, but Caroline thought I wanted ice. Dang, I thought. At the very least she could understand me. She is a nurse, so she should be used to people like me with a dry mouth who has had no water for two stinking days, I thought. When she returned with the ice, I only smiled.

"Hello Reagan," Dr. Gummy declared. "The operation was successful. I predict you will be walking again in no time. But first, please be careful with your leg. The wound is only being held together by a few stitches. Over the course of a few weeks, the nurses and I will tell you how to properly take care of the tender area."

I only nodded my head off, trying to listen without being distracted. The nurse turned TV was on when she was talking to me, and a new episode of my favorite show was on. This time, the adorable Phillip Joe Friend was slaying a dragon!

I was still watching the TV when Nilly, Ms. Grande and Poppy walked in. They all looked as if they hadn't slept a wink, and I could tell Ms. Grande was fuming.

"I'm glad you are alright. How is your leg?" Nilly asked, relieved I hadn't died.

"Yes, how are you? Is your pillow fluffy enough? Are you warm? Are you eating enough? Are you even alive? Are you sleeping fine?" Poppy questioned me. I laughed, since I did expect this coming from her.

"Es oo all," I answered. I meant to say "Yes to all," but my mouth was still dry. Poppy laughed-actually laughed. It was magical for me to see my dear sister smile.

After about an hour or so of "talking" and hanging out, the nurse escorted my guests out of the bare hospital room. I sat back and took a nap and dreamt about being reunited with my parents, and us being and actually positively true family again!

Ms. Grande came back awhile later, still in the bad mood she was in earlier when she visited me.

"Reagan, we need to talk," she stated in a strict voice.

"Look, Ms. Grande, I am truly sorry. I suppose I wanted to see my parents again, but obviously it will never happen. How about you take me home, and I'll help around the house to pay for the hospital bill," I interrupted her.

"No. After you heal, you will go and find your parents. As long as you don't die, I'm fine with you going out and saving your own little world.

"Are you sure?"

"Yes."

"Thank you so much, Ms. Grande."

She went away, and as she did I smiled to myself. The air smelled sweet to me, yet it did not the few days I had been here. I was going to catch my parents, and we were going to be a family again.

Forever.

For dinner I had mashed potatoes, jello and chicken noodle soup. I didn't eat much of it at all; I wasn't very hungry. On the news there was an article about two criminals, a woman and a man who would sneak into houses and stealing all of the jewelry you owned. On some occasions, they would murder you with a knife that was engraved with the date March 25, 2009 and a bloody oak handle with two faces on it. I felt sick. The knife was in my leg. Unless they made multiple knives, that would of been the only one.

My parents were only going to get worse, not better. And poor Nilly was out on her own, catching them herself unless the Smithton Police Department canceled that mission until further notice. But more people would get hurt if they did, and there was one person I knew they would target since I loved her.

Poppy Green.

Chapter 16 - Dr. Gummy's Good News

Two weeks later-

"Run." I urged myself. "Run Reagan! You will die if you don't."

They were right behind me. Screeching, slithering, and howling. I turned a left, and I was back where I had started. This maze was a never ending terror.

"Find her." I was getting angry at myself. Poppy was somewhere in this mess, and I couldn't find her. She could be dead. I thought to myself.

I stopped and turned around. There was nothing behind me, but I knew they were still there. In all the tall limestone walls, I knew they were watching me. Watching me closely. As I thought this, a swarm of them attacked me from behind, and the world I knew changed into an empty, desolate black.

Now-

I cuddled up against the teddy bear Lydia had sent me. I had a vision, and I knew it would come true. I still could feel the souls slithering down my spine and every time I closed my darting eyes, I could see the shallow faces and transparent skin of the empty souls that all died without any chance of purpose in life.

It was now 2:00 am, and the nightmare awoke me. I had a stinging sensation that Poppy would be in danger, but that was impossible. The girl was very safe at Ms. Grande's house, which is only about two miles away from the police station.

Dr. Gummy strolled in and greeted me with a cheery "Hello" the next day. The sun was shining through my small hospital room window, and it was a beautiful day.

"We have good news for you Ms. Reagan," he chirped, sounding like a bird.

"What is it?" I asked, curious of what it could be.

"You only will have to stay here in the hospital for another two days. After that, you will only have to come back in two weeks to get the stitches out, but it will be quite a while to get that cast of yours off."

Finally! I wouldn't have to spend any more boring, useless days in this bare room that they treat me in.

"Thank you!" I exclaimed.

Dr. Gummy just smiled and nodded. "Please be aware of injuring your leg again. Your bone is very delicate, and the cast will not protect it very well. I'd stay away from your job for a while, so you can go to bed rest for a few months at the very least."

Dang. I had hoped that I could of jumped right in and find my parents, but according to Gummy Bear (which is my nickname for Dr. Gummy), I have to rest. In bed. For months at a time! And if that doesn't make the situation worse, I'll have to learn how to walk and run when I get the cast off of my leg.

Once again, Poppy and Nilly came by to visit me. They brought flowers which the nurses took away for sanitation purposes. They smelled sweet, changing the old, dry smell in the cramped room for once.

"Hey, Reagan, how's your leg?" Poppy asked, obviously concerned about it.

"Oh, the same old leg," I replied.

I just want to say I'm sorry for not speaking up to...her. It was my fault you got stabbed," Nilly apologized.

"No. If you had stood up to my mother, she would have killed you. I don't want that to happen, considering that you are my only friend," I reassured the sorry girl.

"Reagan Lucille, it was my fault."

My response was laughing at her for using my middle name.

"Hey, it's difficult for me already to apologize to you, but when you laugh it only makes it worse."

"Sorry," I giggled and then soon the whole room was erupting in side-splitting laughter.

"It's *giggle* not *snort* funny!" Nilly complained. Poppy and I were to focused on stopping our roaring, compared to listening to Nilly apologize.

```
Chapter 17 - My Old Man
```

One of the nurses helped me into an old, antique wheelchair that squeaked when she rolled it. Ms. Grande walked with us, as Dr. Gummy handed her a packet of all the information I needed to take care of my leg. He already told me, but I forgot so he typed up an information sheet "Just for me."

Ms. Grande's huge van was waiting for us in the hospital parking lot. Dr. Gummy slid the big door open with ease, and everyone helped to lift me into a seat. Once I was situated, they all put the wheelchair beside me. Ms. Grande started the engine, and we carefully drove away from the brick hospital that towered over us. When I looked back, the crowd was walking into the sliding doors.

"Are you going to miss the hospital?" Ms. Grande asked me.

"No, not really. It was a little bit of a bore for me."

"I understand."

I nodded as she got onto the freeway that would take us to her house. As the car slowly rocked back and forth, my eyes closed and my breathing became gentle, almost like it was nonexistent, but my shallow breaths were still alive.

"Ah!" The sun glared into my delicate eyes as I slowly opened them. I was in the room that I had slept in before I became a police officer. The lime green walls unfortunately reflected the sunlight, making it look brighter than it actually was. I looked at the alarm clock on the bedside table, and it flashed before my eyes 11:47. I groaned. Although I got a full night's rest, I still felt tired and I ached. I swung my feet around the bed and slipped into the wheelchair the hospital gladly donated to me. I rolled my way out of the best room and into the hallway, when I abruptly stopped. The stairs. Which I had forgotten about.

"Help!" I called to no one in particular, but I needed someone's help.

"Oh, Reagan, are you awake?" Poppy asked me, coming out of her room.

"Yes, Poppy," I replied in an irritated voice.

"Someone has a temper," she mocked me.

"Don't poke the bear."

"Yes ma'am," she joked to me.

"Ms. Grande," I called "Can you help me get down the stairs?"

"Ms. Grande isn't here. She went to go get groceries."

"Oh."

"She will be back soon."

"How soon?"

"I don't know. She left about ten minutes ago, and said she would be back in thirty."

"Can you call her?"

"She didn't leave us anything to contact her with. Maybe we could send her a letter in the mail?"

"Haha, very funny Poppy."

"No, I'm serious."

"As serious as an ostrich."

"Whatever, Reagan."

We went downstairs to play Monopoly, and we played about two more rounds before we began to grow concerned.

"Do you want to walk down to the gas station down the street and call her from their phone?" I asked.

"Sure. It has been about an hour since she left. Maybe something happened to her."

We put on our coats and Poppy pushed me to the station, which was about a five minute walk. We got inside and I instantly felt that something was off. I glanced around as my palms began to sweat.

"You know what, Poppy? How about we wait at the house."

"Why should we? Ms. Grande isn't where she is supposed to be. We need to call her."

"I know. I guess I just have this peculiar feeling that something bad will happen.

"We are safe. Nobody goes to this gas station anyway."

Poppy navigated us to the telephone, which was near the bathrooms. Poppy dialed the number I told her, and we waited for Ms. Grande to answer, but she never did.

"Maybe she didn't reach her phone in time?" Poppy suggested, although we both knew she was wrong.

"I think she is doing this for a reason," I announced. Poppy nodded, and turned the wheelchair around. As we headed for the exit, a dark mysterious figure approached us.

"Nice to see you again, Reagan. Your mother told me that you have been a bad girl. Is that true?"

"Who are you?" I asked him.

"Your old man, of course," he replied.

"Dad?!" Poppy exclaimed. I widened my eyes in shock, since the last time I had encountered one of my parents, things hadn't gone so well. I tried to conceal my shock and anger, but I could tell that my dad noticed, yet he did not say anything.

"Poppy, stay out of this," I warned her, my voice shaking.

"Poppy, you have really grown up," my father started "you are a work of art. Poppy, you would look extraordinary in a white dress, with your hair in a bun and-"

"Leave her alone," I demanded. As I said that, my father crept behind my wheelchair, and I heard Poppy scream.

"Poppy!" I twisted my neck so I could look behind me, but no one was there.

No one was there.

I slipped out of my wheelchair and lay on the ground, sobbing. My one sister, gone. How could I live without her? She is who I am and who I will be.

"Are you okay?" I heard a women ask me. I looked up, and saw her lean down towards me. "Are you okay?" she asked again, this time with sympathy.

"My sister sniff was kid- kidnaped sniff by my dad," I wailed to the women.

"Oh sweetie I am sorry. I should have known that the screaming I heard was your sister's. I am so sorry. The police will find her. I am sure of it. My son is an officer. He has won-"

I started crying again, knowing that trying to find her would be close to impossible. I had lost my sister. We had spent our lives together, and we never, ever parted. All of the memories we had spent together I would have to forget because of the pain. The everlasting pain.

Once again I broke into a fit of tears, and the woman dialed 911 on her cell phone. By now I had lured a crowd of people.

"Yes, a little girl has been kidnapped…"

Chapter 18 - Run Away?

Two weeks later-

I twisted and turned around, trying to get the empty souls off of me. I jumped up, shook them off and ran through the maze. They screech behind me as a turned a left, and another left. I stopped, looking at the silver cage that I closed my sister.

"Poppy!" I exclaimed, both happy and relieved. "There you are."

"No, Reagan. It's a trap. Run away and never come for me again."

"How is it a trap?

"Go. Go away and please, never return or bad things will happen."

"What bad things?"

"Mom and dad didn't say, but I know that they are bad."

I ran was, tearing at my clothes. The bits and pieces fell on the floor wave, when all the sudden I was in a field of vibrant red Poppies.

"Oh no," I whispered as if I was talking to someone about something confidential and secret.

They started releasing a gas similar to the one they gave me in my hospital. Except this gas was obviously deadlier, and much more advanced.

I covered my mouth with my thin shirt, and ran towards an old colonial house that look as if it could fall into a pile of rubble. I tripped, and I couldn't get up.

Now-

I held the cup of warm hot chocolate in my hand as I weeped on Ms. Grande's shoulder. My eyes cloudy and hands clammy, she patted my back and I could sense that she was also scared and terrified like I was. The poor woman sobbed with me, also gripping another cup of hot chocolate she made for us. We held on to each other for about ten short minutes before we let go and separated.

The sunshine crept through the faded black curtains that were hung up on the only window in the room. I opened my crusty eyes and then remembered what had happened the day before. Poppy.

Since she was very obedient, I had a feeling that my parents would try and turn her into them.

The people they are. The bad and ugly people my parents changed themselves to be.

I shook my head. If I was going to save her, I would need to join back on the police. Now.

Even if that meant running away.

I scooted myself to the very edge of the bed, and carefully stood and evenly distributed my weight on both legs. I instantly felt pain shooting up my right leg and fell over onto the bed.

"Try again," I coaxed myself. This time, I only put all of my weight on my left leg, and then I slowly transferred it to my right. That was much better. I took a big step forward, and fell over. I had to try for about all of the morning, when I was finally capable of walking around the bedroom as if I were a pro at it.

I ambled down the stairs and opened the kitchen door. Since Ms. Grande she was working, I knew this was my one and only chance to run away. The tile felt cold on my left foot. I looked around for the biggest knife possible, and there it was. Gleaming and shimmering, its blade was easily a good 8" inches and the wood handle was polished in such a way it made the whole scene look as if it were made by a master knife maker. I slipped it out of the base it was held in, and I grasped the handle.

Upstairs, I sat on the floor and forced the knife under the thick cast, and sliced downwards. A bolt of air rushed into the linen as I peeled it off, layer by layer.

My leg was an unnatural pale, surprising me since I had it on for such a short time period. The skin around the stab wound was swollen and pussing. I couldn't see the actual wound itself, since it was covered up in a bandage. Curiously I lightly brushed my fingertips onto the bandage, and it stung. "Ouch." I crawled over to the bed and pulled myself up. Once again, I stood up. There was astonishingly no pain at all, except for a few stings and burns here and there. I slowly inched my foot forward, preparing myself for my "first baby steps," just as I did like I was a baby again. I then lifted my foot awkwardly off the ground, and flapped my leg forward. I then did the same with my other leg, and switched off between the two.

 With the help on a cane I found in the master bedroom, I was soon able to amble across my room, down the hall and into the bathroom and back. Slowly, I let go of the wooden handle attached to it and then I tried walking without it. I soon became tired, and used the cane to climb down the stairs. I then got an old canvas bag that Ms. Grande used for groceries, climbed back up the stairs, packed clothing, bathroom essentials, bandages and my emergency stash of $347. I went down the staircase again and packed food and water bottles. I wrote a note on a notepad for Ms. Grande-

Dear Ms. Grande,

I am going off to find Poppy. I hope you don't mind. Please don't call the police because I need to be the first one who finds my sister. I am also sorry for stealing most of your food, water bottles and bandages. If I know my parents, they would totally hide somewhere in plain sight.

Thanks for everything, Reagan Lucille Green

P.S, I took off my cast, so if you see a big kitchen knife and leg-sized cast on the floor of the bedroom I stayed in, don't worry. I have a foolproof plan.

P.P.S, I also took the cane with the wooden handle with me. If you need it back, keep in mind that you will get it back when I find Poppy.

I put the note on the refrigerator, and held it in place with a magnet with a rainbow on it. At this moment I noticed another note on the fridge. Oh. My. Gosh. It was from my parents. The blue piece of paper shook in my hands as I read it.

So, Reagan. As you know, your priceless sister is with us. We know where you are - and always will. we will write you notes hinting where we are. Here is the first clue:

It flows gently, never stopping. It cries all the time, but tears never fall.

Lots of love, mom and dad

P.s Poppy is very safe. In case you were worried about her .

P.p.s you only have a month to find Poppy.

I knew where to go. In the outskirts of our small, unknown town there is a silk store, and they advertise their products by showing the silk "weeping" about how it is "lonely." I honestly don't understand why they do it, but the business is doing well so I guess the concept is working.

The only way to get there was to call up Nilly and ask her to drive me. Since I couldn't stand being in the last place Poppy was, I'd have to go to the wine market about two blocks away and call Nilly there. She wrote down her phone number for me at the hospital so in case I needed to call her, I could reach her. After digging through many coat pockets including the old, red sweatshirt I was wearing, I found it in my ugly hot pink jacket.

My walk down to the wine market took about ten minutes. I hobbled my way inside, and made my way back to the public telephone. I dialed her number, and I waited. She finally answered, but she thought I was someone else.

"Tim, stop calling me. I've told you before, our relationship is over. Stop," she hissed in an irritated voice.

"Nilly, it's me, Reagan. I'm not Tod or whoever he was," I reassured her.

"Oh, Reagan. I'm so sorry. Tim and I have had a past going way back. I broke up with him in third grade. That was like, ten years ago."

"That's okay. I have a favor to ask you."

"Sure, what is it?"

"My sister was kidnapped by... them and I was wondering if you could pick me up and take me to Silk City?"

"First of all, sure. And second, you can say that "them" are your parents. Although I will admit that having your mother stab you in the leg with a knife and kidnapping my younger sister would do a number on me. Not that I have a sister."

"Great, thanks."

"Where are you now?"

"I am embarrassed to say, but at the wine market."

"Ha, that is great. I love it."

"It's not funny! It was the closest telephone available."

"What are you doing there? Buying wine? Or are you lying to me... again?"

"You shut up. Come and grab me before I'm the one kidnapped."

"Bye."

I hung the phone up, strolled outside and sat down on a bench by the one stoplight in town. I was waiting for about fifteen minutes before Nilly pulled over onto the sidewalk. In Smithton, nobody used the sidewalks since nobody lived there. I'm not kidding. The population was around 920.

I opened up the door, stepped in and buckled my seatbelt. Nilly smiled at me in a sad way and backed away from the sidewalk.

"So, how is the police thing going for you?" I asked Nilly, hoping to spark a conversation.

"Actually, since I had quote ''been through alot,'' they are letting me on a break until you get better."

"Cool. Anyway, I owe you an apology. I feel bad for lying. I really shouldn't have. I'm sorry."

"It is fine. I have lied a couple of times myself in my life. I can see how you feel about your parents being criminals and all that junk, but I will admit I was a bit mad when I found out and-"

"Thank you very much! A hundred pounds just came off of my shoulders!" I thanked her.

After around ten minutes of driving, we reached a small outdoor mall.

"Silk City is in there. Thanks for driving me," I acknowledged.

"Wait... I never said I wasn't going with you."

Oh thank goodness. To be honest, I was scared about going in the mall. Knowing my parents, this was about the time where they would trick me. I was hurt emotionally and physically, my sister was kidnapped, and to top that all off, I had run away from my guardian. I could imagine that they would do something else to me.

We strolled around the mall for a while, looking into windows of stores. All the sudden, the door to Silk City and their cheesy advertisements were face-to-face with me. Nilly was soon behind me, and in unison we pushed the heavy doors open. Or in our case, as open as we could push them.

"We are looking for a handwritten note that is blue. It should say something like a clue on it. I expect my parents left it in plain sight. Keep in mind although there is limited space in the store, to my parents there is unlimited space," I reported to Nilly in a soft whisper. Her only response was a nod, and we started looking.

I looked in the clothing section and found nothing. I then moved onto the cloth area, where again I found not one trace of a blue note. Nilly and I met up, revealing that I, nor Nilly had found any note. We sat down to regather ourselves, when I spotted it.

There it was. I stared at it, adoring the blue cardstock, then I realized where it was. Glued to the front of a customer's shopping bag. The woman who carried it was now walking out of the store. Nilly and I nodded, and walked up to the woman.

"Hello. I am Nilly and this is Reagan. We work at the Smithton Police Department and our mission is to find two criminals. They have started to write us notes, and couldn't help noticing that one of them is pasted onto your bag," Nilly explained. Sure enough, the woman looked surprised to see the blue note addressed to me. She ripped it off, threw it at us and strutted away like she was better than us. I scrambled to pick it up off of the gum-stained cement. I grasped it, and opened it.

```
Dear Reagan,

We couldn't help noticing that
you got that girl to help you
again. And also, nice move at
the wine market. That was a
comedy show for us. Now, your
clue:

Sticks and stones may break your
bones, but we all know where you
can find sticks and stones.

Xoxo, mommy and daddy
```

"Sticks and stones? That would be the...Riverfalls Forest? Wouldn't it be?" I asked Nilly. Riverfalls Forest is known to be a very stony forest. If you ever hiked there, you would have to be cautious for rocks along the trails.

"I guess."

"Do you want to go?"

"If we want to catch your parents."

Clutching the note, we drove away towards Riverfalls Forest, which was a few hours away. On the drive there, we talked about what we would do when we got there.

"Let's just say that we are going hiking, we pretend to get lost, head over to whatever the 'stones' are, and catch them.

"Sounds like a plan."

Chapter 19- Float and Fall

After four long hours of driving, we finally spotted a sign that mentioned the forest. We took the exit, and pulled into the road that lead to the entrance. A few mountains around toward over us, as she guided the old vehicle to a stop. In front of us was where we would get passes to go hiking.

"Hello, two hiking tickets please."

The woman in the little wooden ticket shack in the middle of the road held out a receipt, and Nilly handed her the money that we owed to the lady. We drove down another mile or so before we found a parking lot, Nilly parked her car and we found one of the many trails that led to Mt. Sacher, which was the tallest mountain in the forest. Compared to Mt. Everest, it was a hill. The peak was 1,293ft, and it was off-limits. The highest you could climb was 1,000ft.

I climbed it once with my family, but it was too hard for my six year old legs.

We set off on one of the trails, which was rocky and rough. Nilly and I brought all of the food and water we had, what wasn't very much.

Up, up, up we climbed, and the higher we got, the more my bad leg hurt. The cane was starting to wear and bend, and then all the sudden it snapped, lunging me to the side of the trail, making it dangerous. There was a steep decline right in front of me, so if I did fall, I would probably break a bone. If not, I would injure my leg more.

I held onto a tree branch, but I felt it bend, and then it snapped. I went tumbling down the steep incline next to me and landed in a warm, burbling stream.

I felt that something was off, I smelled something sweet, like honey. I remembered my Aunt Vera on my father's side owned a bee farm before she died of cancer. For our family, honey is bad luck. I still ignored the feeling, and started sipping the too-sweet water. Man that felt good. The water soothed my throat, and calmed that fiery feeling to go away.

"Reagan! Are you okay?" Nilly stumbled behind me.

"Yeah. Although I do feel as if I broke my leg. Again."

"And also, with your bad leg, you may not want to try and climb back on the trail. I would recommend that we walk down here for a while."

"Can we please sit here for a while?"

"Sure. We have been walking for over an hour."

To rest my exhausted leg, I took a nap until I was awoken by an odd sound.

>Grrrrrrrrrrrrr... grrrrrrrrrr... grrrrrr.

I looked behind me and there sat a grizzly bear. She was big; bigger than any other bear I had ever saw. The brownish-black fur swayed in the wind, and she growled at me. The honey air now went sour, as I slowly got up, and backed away. I then remembered Nilly, who was asleep in the dense grass.

"Nilly," I whispered to her, trying to get her to wake up. She stirred, and groaned. Prints of grass were on her cheek, and she quickly got up, and spotted the bear as the bear saw her.

"Don't move." I once again spoke quietly to her, but she started screaming. I grabbed the backpack and ran, leaving Nilly for the bear to harass. I ran into the dense woods, as I heard screaming in the background. Once it stopped, I tip-toed back to the camp out, and Nilly was gone.

Oh thank goodness. I thought, thankful she had escaped. Or so I thought, until I smelled blood and raw meat. I glanced around looking for the bear, but there was no sign of her.

And I saw the fresh pile of human bones with a blue note taped to the skull.

```
Dear Reagan,

You may have noticed the bear.
We are proud to say that we are
now in control of the forest,
and the maze you will be
entering soon! Anyway, as you
know, your father was a
veterinarian for a while, and he
created that bear himself!
Aren't you proud of him?

Your clue: float and fall.
```

I read in disgust. I threw the cardstock on the ground, and stomped on it. Nilly. She was murdered by my parents. My only friend. My only friend. She was gone. She was actually truly gone. As in she would never come back. She would never come back. If she would never return to the world we live in, I should at least bury her remains in the soil.

Using my bare hands, I dug a hole deep enough to heap onto each other, and tenderly pushed them in, one by one. Then I filled the hole in with the dirt I had pulled out of the ground. I fished around in my sweatshirt pocket and found a piece of chipped granite that I had found while hiking, and put it on the grave, and said a quick prayer.

I grabbed Nilly's phone, which was throw off in a patch of grass. I would use it for an emergency, and to call the real cops when I defeated my parents. I also snatched all of the food and water, looked back at Nilly's grave on last time, and slumped away. Tears rolled down as I did this, but I had to do this. Nilly would want me to carry on without her, yet my heart ached as I thought this.

According to the note, I had to float. I guessed it meant the stream, but I didn't know how to fall. I started to walk beside the stream, since I didn't want to get my leg wet.

The stream carried on for what seemed like miles, and again my leg started to hurt and burn. I sat down on a small rock and this time I didn't fall asleep, since the last time I did someone died.

Chapter 20- Chain

Eventually the stream stopped, and so did I. For two days, I had been walking nonstop without any sleep, and I hadn't found any clues from my parents. This was a chance for me to catch my breath. I heard footsteps behind me, and when I turned around no one was there. I turned back around, towards the gently flowing stream, and that was when I felt something hit the back of my head. I blacked out into a darkness that felt like I was falling.

I awoke in a dark room, with no light source. Not one window, nothing. From what I could tell, I was chained up in a chair. "Hello," I called out to anyone who could save me. My voice echoed all around me, so this meant I was in a big room.

A light flickered on, and I screamed. But it was only Poppy. "Poppy!" I exclaimed, wrapping my sore arms around her. Her hair was a mess, and she was dressed in a pale blue dress that looked beautiful on her. She seemed to cry, and as she did this she gasped for air. I looked into her blue eyes, but they were not blue anymore. They were gray - the color she hated the most. Poppy always had looked delicate, but this time her skin looked as it was porcelain. As I hugged her, I felt pieces of glass in her skin. No, they were growing on her. She only handed me a blue note, and disappeared into thin air. I couldn't read it. I didn't want to read it. What I had seen shocked me.

Was Poppy turning into something?

In the low light I read the note she handed me anyway, although it was the thing I did not want to do at all:

```
Dear Reagan,

We have something to tell you.
There are two Poppys now! Your
genius father cloned her, and
the only way to tell who is who:
the pieces of invisible glass in
her skin.. Oh, and by the way,
you can only make contact with
her nine more times because
slowly but surely Poppy is
ejecting a poison into your
bloodstream because the glass is
a special Glass. And there is no
cure. Just thought you wanted to
know.

Toodles, mom and dad
```

Wow. My parents are great. Murdering my best friend, innocent people and not to mention, threatening to kill me more than once. I knew I should quit, but I couldn't. Poppy was in danger, my parents murdered multiple people. They were just. Too. Dangerous.

My hands scratched against the tight chain that forced me against the cold, metal chair. I quickly searched for a dent in one of the many loops to help me break free. A magician that did magic at my 5th birthday taught me how to escape, and I kept that info for years tucked away just in case…

"Happy birthday to you, happy birthday to you, happy birthday dear Reagan, happy birthday to you, cha-cha-cha!" My family sang to me since I wasn't very good at making friends. Only a girl named Suzanne showed up at my house with her younger brother Ralph, but she was ten years old and very self-centered. Ralph wasn't as bad, but he could still be pretty stuck up. My parents knew their parents, so that's how she ended up on 364 Newfound Road on my fifth birthday.

Since I was five, I didn't care about not having anyone to play with. I didn't care about having nobody to trade snacks behind the teacher's back, even though it wasn't allowed.

Or nobody to have over when dad was working late night, and wasn't at home. I really honestly truly didn't care about not having anyone to whisper in my ear during nap time, and I didn't care that I would respond back to them, only and surely if I ever would be a friend to someone. A friend to anyone, for that matter. Even Jamie Sullivan, the weird kid who picked his nose, and ate butterflies for fun.

The magician came over at exactly 2:25. He was five minutes early, and he had a curly mustache, a black velveteen top hat, a brown, musty coat that had been patched quite a few times, and a red bow tie that had yellow stains on it. I noticed the stains, so I came up to Mr. Ferguson, which was his name and asked him, "Do you like mustard?"

"No, little girl, why do you ask the great, all powerful magician Ferguson?"

"You have yellow stains on your tie, Mr. Great All Powerful Ferguson," I responded to his booming voice. Mr. Ferguson's pale face reddened, and I giggled, for pestering him was a carousel for me.

"Why don't you go find the birthday girl Ruth, and tell her that I'm here."

"Her name is Reagan, and I am her...cousin Lucille Alli Karen Isabel Hanna?" He groaned, and rubbed his temples, as I pranced up the stairs, put on a pink poofy dress and shiny black flats with butterflies on them. I sprinted downstairs, and into my parents bathroom I went. I opened the drawer that kept my mother's makeup, and opened a tubed on hot pink lipstick. I applied it to my lips gently, knowing that my mother loves her makeup. I adorned my wrists with my mother's newest jewelry collection, and sashayed down the hall, slowly.

"Hello, Mr. Great All Powerful Ferguson," I chirped when I reached to where he was setting up for the performance.

"Who are you?" He asked, eying me.

"Me? Oh, you should know!" I emphasized, batting my eyelashes at him. *"I am Reagan! My cousin sent me!"*

"Look, little girl. Please get me the real Reagan. I don't have time for this," Mr. Ferguson grumped. I widened my eyes for effect, and said, *"But I am the real Reagan. You don't believe me?"*

"Stop playing this stupid game of yours. You are driving me nuts, and not to mention,

the show starts in 16 seconds." I used my amazing acting skills to wail and scream, "Mommy! Mr. Great All Powerful Ferguson sad a bad word! He said the 's' word to me! The 's' word! I repeat! The 's' word. Oh, do you want me to say it?" At this point on my carousel ride, my mother had run from the kitchen to the dining room, where the magician and I stood. "He said stupid! That is what he said!" My mother looked at him, as he rubbed his temples for the third time today. (While I was ranting about the 's' word, he didn't rub- he rubbed his temples. I swear, if rubbing your temples was an Olympic sport, he would win four gold medals, he was that good.)

My mother eventually worked everything out with Mr. Ferguson. He would pay her $0.50 for "cursing," and she told him that. I really was Reagan.   The show went on, and I remember every time he looked at me, he glared. So I glared back at him when he did so to me.

"Hello, children," Mr. Ferguson said in a mysterious voice, even though there were only three children in the room: Me, Suzanne and Ralph, who was six. "Today I will show you the wonders of the world by doing magic," and he fluttered his fingers as he said this. I frowned as

Suzanne roll her light green eyes, so I shoved her just a bit. She cried out loud, and I ignored her.

Mr. Ferguson started the magic show with card games that were fascinating, and then some hat tricks. I will say, although I was the birthday girl, he never chose me to be his volunteer. Even though I raised my hand the highest, he and his mustard-stained tie didn't care one bit. Even though I sat in a perfect crisscross applesauce, while Suzanne and Ralph were laying on the floor. Even though I sat quietly, (well, I had to tape my mouth to keep me from talking) Mr. Ferguson didn't pick me. Suzanne and Ralph were complaining really, really, really loud. Then, my tides changed. Mr. Ferguson asked me to volunteer! He pulled out a cold, metal chair from his bag, and a very long chain, that sparkled every time it moved. "Can you sit down, Reagan?" He asked me. I watched his mustache grow into a wide grin that even now makes me shiver.

"Sure can-do, Mr. Great All Powerful Ferguson. I will sit right smack in the middle," I responded to him. I plopped down onto the cold metal, as I shivered. Not only was the metal cold, I felt unusually cold.

Slowly, Mr. Ferguson wrapped the chain around my knobby little legs. Up, up, up he went until the chain was draped onto my shoulders. He secured the shining chain with a lock, and spoke to the 'audience.'

"Reagan here is chained to this chair with a ginormous lock without a key. I will break her from the chair, without unnaturally breaking the chain." He nodded towards me and kneeled down to be my height, then Mr. Ferguson whispered in my ear, and told me a set of instructions, which were "Not to be told to anyone." I started to do them, and I heard him talk to the audience. Where is that dent he was talking about? I thought to myself. Every single chain has them, he had told me. I rubbed my dainty little fingers around more, and felt a single dent the size of a needle's diameter. I put both of my thumbs into the hole, and very slightly, it sliced open just enough to pull the whole chain apart. It slipped down to my shiny shoes, and I stood up. I heard applause from my mom, dad, Poppy and even Suzanne. I felt proud. I now knew how to escape from any chain!

Chapter 21- Dolor Aegritudo In Ocul Familia De La Grene.

The light flickered off yet again, and in the dark I sat in the chair. My thumbs searched frantically for a little dent or imperfection-anything I could use to escape and go save Poppy. I finally found a small cavity, which was even smaller than the one I worked with when I was five. I squeezed the tips of my fingernails into the extremely small hole, and spread them apart. Crack. The chain broke apart, and as I stood up, heard a squeak from my footsteps, and I fell into a deep, dark scary hole as my broken heart pounded into the darkness below.

I fell on a soft substance, as I was still shaking from the fall, which had scared me. I looked around, and noticed that I was on a hill, seeing miles and miles of rock. It almost twisted and turned itself into a maze, like the ones at the pumpkin patch. I squinted into the stormy red and black horizon, and recognized that it was still growing, like it was having its own little growth spurt. It was a never ending, infinite city, almost, and I knew this was the maze that my parents had built, and where they were hiding.

The walls were a beautiful clean white color, it sparkled even though there was no sunlight and it was raining hard. The grass was a beautiful green and well-kept. The sign in front of the entrance to the maze was engraved in a swirled marble, and it read Dolor Aegritudo In Ocul Familia De La Grene. I looked around for any clues about my parents or Poppy, but there wasn't any. I strolled along the grass, marveling at the 20 feet walls, and appeared before me was a blue note, but I didn't pick it up and read it. Instead I passed it, as I were in a trance. Then all of the sudden, I remarked at the dazzling entrance to the maze. Gargoyles like the ones I saw at Notre Dame when I went to France decorated the big opening, and a blood-red curtain swayed in the wind.

This is where Poppy is, I thought to myself as I barely stepped onto the stone bricks that sat into the grass. On them where names, and dates. These must be gravestones. I remembered the time when I was at my father's uncle's funeral. The graves were exactly in this order, because after the bland service Poppy and I went over to the part of the cemetery where Uncle Stephan wasn't buried. We remarked at the hilarious names engraved on the granite gravestones. Petunia Wilde, Tutu Louse, Bob McMuff, Jilly Gene, Harrisold Rubric jr, Oxford Petty. We giggled as the names flew out of our mouths, and snorted every once in awhile when we would spot an extra weird name such as Karisoul Marisa Floofellberrieh. And now, lying before me was a copy of the grave I had been in so many years ago. With Poppy, should I add.

I took yet another step forward, but it was as if an invisible force field threw me back, towards the blue card stock note my ugly parents had written.

```
         Dear Reagan,

We are sorry to inform you, but
this is the last note we will
send to you, little girl. But,
on the bright side, you have
found the maze! After you are
done reading this, you will
enter Dolor Aegritudo In Ocul
Familia De La Grene! Aren't you
excited? We certainly are…

Here is your last clue:

Enter the maze, and you will
wander as days go by, even
decades

But finding Poppy is the key

To seeing
```

But beware, dear,

Every corner you turn is another level of fear

You can run, but cannot hide,

For thousands of beady eyes

Watch you as you and only you pass by.

If you run out of food,

Better find it fast

Because in this maze it surely will not last

Your clue to Poppy is walking, little 'ne,

For not a day will pass if you do not walk or run

Seeking shelter is hard, you see

But you have to do this, no turning back now

If you only turn right turns, you will see sacrifice on your soul

Only left turns, slaughter behold

```
If you do it right, you will see
A silver cage, standing before thee
With your beloved Poppy.

Hope that doesn't help!
Kisses, Mom and Dad
```

I closed the note and the same invisible force field that carried me away from the maze now jerked me to it. The tall, red curtain parted itself just enough for me to walk through, and very slowly, very carefully I did. The polished granite gravestones clicked as I walked on them, just as my own steps did back at the police station.

My heart was pounding, my palms were sweating knowing that I would probably die. Click. Click. Click. My head throbbed, but I couldn't stop. Anything could happen now, Nilly was dead, my parents were murderers, and Poppy was kidnapped and a prisoner to my mom and dad. I was all alone, and my parents knew that. They knew I was scared, upset and angry. They knew all along, before I was a police officer. My own mother and father gave birth to me, so they could eventually kill me in my later life.

If that was the case, I would kill them.

Don't turn right, and don't turn left, I thought to myself. The entrance to the maze was now sealed, and it was disappearing into a tiny dot that I had to squint to see. By now, I had been walking for about thirty minutes, and was already getting worn down and exhausted. The walls echoed off my tiptoes, since the gravestones were still going on. Once or twice I had spotted a familiar name. My LaLa was one of them.

I turned a right, and heard peculiar shuffling behind me, yet when I turned around, nothing was there. I took two more steps, and the shuffling persisted. A smell arose, a wood, like the smell of the chess pieces I used to play with Luke, my second best friend, who I had met in third grade. He loved to play chess, and shared that with me. While the people around us played whatnot during recess (tag wasn't the trend yet), Luke taught me chess. He would bring his chess wooden set to school, and we would play, play, play…

"Do you play?" asked a boy with stringy black hair and big, green eyes that smiled to me.

"Play what?" I asked him back, not knowing what he was referring to. I was swinging on the rusty swings on the playground after school, when my parents were late to pick me up. The boy motioned me to follow, and he led me to a bench. There sat a wooden chess set, all set up. I marveled over the delicate little pieces, as Luke explained to me what they were and what their purpose was.

I played with him a little bit, getting used to the feeling.

"No, you can't make that move. That's a pawn. You can only move forward." he brushed against my hand as he moved the small piece to where I had originally put it. We giggled, and began to chase each other around the playground. Both of us were dogging slides and avoiding the swings until his mother arrived in a tight tan dress and bright red high heels. Her black hair that matched Luke's was curled, and her eyes were hidden by sunglasses that sparkled in the sun that had been shining that day.

"Come on Luke. The chef has to keep our food warm, and time won't help him," she

bossed in a high pitched squeaky voice that almost made me cover my ears. "Time also will not help me with my wrinkles, either," she sighed. Luke sadly picked up his chess set and put it in the wooden box it came in. he slumped away as I waved goodbye to him. He was muttering to himself, as if he despised his mother's sassiness.

His mother grabbed hold of his hand, and strutted away quicker than Luke could walk. "Slow down, mother," he complained and she ignored him. They walked to their slick, red car that was parked in a handicapped spot, and drove away. I could still tell that they were still arguing, and I dashed back to the rusty swing, and swung until my current foster home, the Sanders family picked me up.

Luke eventually transferred to a very prestigious school called Staple Academy School. This was about two months later, so our friendship was very brief, yet I still remember the smell of Luke's chess set.

The shuffling became quicker and quicker, as I walked faster and faster. I turned another corner, knowing that doing that action would not help me at all. I turned back, heart pounding, when I saw it. The details were enormous, with a crown etched into her head.

The queen piece in a chess set. Luke's chess set, to be exact. The figure wore a black robe, with small crystals glued to it.

I started running knowing that the queen would always be following me; she could travel anywhere on a chessboard, killing off any of her opponents. In this game, I was the opponent. Just as I thought this, the floor turned into a chessboard identical to the one I used to play on, with all of the pieces set up exactly how they would be in a normal game. But this game was different, for I was a pawn, the piece that could only move forward and only move one space, not counting your first move.

The pawn directly in front of me jumped ahead two spaces, revealing the queen behind it. The other side's mission wasn't to capture the king; their mission was to kill me.

The pawn on the left of me jumped ahead only one space, not risking its capture. The queen made a move, and now she could make two more moves before capturing me. I decided to stay where I was, and I pushed the pawn on my right side to move ahead one space, so that could hold off the queen for at least three moves. The queen once again moved to position herself to kill me in another way. This time she was right in front of me.

Checkmate, I thought, realizing this was to be my last few minutes on earth. As another pawn was about to make its move, one of the Poppy's, I think the clone Poppy stepped onto the board, and tiptoed behind her highness. Poppy then gave her a big shove.

Bang! Was all I heard when I witnessed a violent flash of red, matching the color of the horizon. The blast was so big, it knocked me over at the very time I saw the chess pieces fade into a vagueness I couldn't explain.

Poppy, who seemed unaffected by the blast went over to help me up as ashes gently floated in the air, probably symbolizing me and Luke's vestige friendship.

Tears rolled down my blackened face, clearing the ashes away from my skin. Poppy kneeled down and lent her hand, which I had refused.

She was still in the pale blue dress she was in earlier, but she wasn't crying and her cheeks had a little bit of color. Like I was, she was covered in ashes that revealed small glass pieces in her skin. They were almost invisible, just as one of my parents' letters had mentioned. I ignored this, and grabbed hold of her hand. I felt a burn, which I had not noticed the first time I had made contact with Clone

Poppy. Still holding hands, I studied her, noticing the way she acted towards me. Her hands were calm, but the real Poppy would never be calm in a situation like this. Instead, she would be frantically running away, cursing herself for getting into it. But Clone Poppy was still my "sister," and she was my only hope of seeing the real Poppy.

The maze seemed to weave on. Left. Right. Right. Left. Left. The turns I made seemed useless, as if I wasn't making any progress whatsoever. Meeting Clone Poppy had raised my spirits, just a little bit. I rounded another corner, and instantly felt someone or something was watching me. The incident with the queen had made me more aware, since I knew my parents would be sending in more "terrors."

The heavy backpack began to ache on my back, but I couldn't stop. Knowing that if I did stop, I would die, so I kept persevering on, towards Poppy.

The sun gently set, letting me know that the day would come to an end, and signaling a tiring and weary night full of walking. My eyes began to close, and I abruptly opened them. The red and black sky was now beautiful shades of purple, and red as the moon peeked out from the artist's dream sky. I got out Nilly's phone to check the time, and the screen read an impossible 6:34. No, I thought to myself. It has to be at least seven o'clock. The sky quickly turned to a bright blue, and the blue dissolved into silence and utter blackness, with the exception of a few stars poking out of the sky. I kept turning around, making sure I wasn't being followed. That night was my first night in the maze, and I didn't want to die.

I then heard a hissing sound behind me, but I ignored it, hoping that my parents were trying to scare me. The hissing continued, as I yelled into the darkness, "You're not scaring me, mom and dad!" All that was responded to me was the hissing, which grew closer than before. My quick walking turned to a run, and the running evolved to a sprint. The ground thumped under me as I sprinted to no safety, for I knew that I was dead this time.

I made a left turn, and before me stood a rickety shack, that looked like it would blow over in the slightest puff of air. I opened the rotting door and stepped inside. The wooden floors were unusually scratched, like an animal had skid across the room. The only piece of furniture there was a metal chair, like the chair I had sat in so many years ago at my fifth birthday party.

My legs were sore for sprinting and walking so much. I heaved myself over, and sat in it. *Hisssssss.* The noise was back, but I could tell it wasn't from outside. It was from the chair.

Chapter 22- In a Field of Red Poppies

I tried to sit up, but I couldn't. The chair wouldn't move, probably because it was nailed to the ground. I forced myself to sit up fast, but the chair held me back. I felt around my waist, feeling for an invisible belt buckle or chain, but there was nothing there. I started to panic, knowing that I was probably going to die.

"Ow!" I yelled, feeling a burning sensation on my back and thighs. For the last time, I tried to sit up and get out of the chair, but once again I wouldn't budge. The burning became stronger, and it spread to my sore back. I cried in pain, regretting my decision to ever become a police officer. The burning became more and more intense, and weeped and weeped for my life.

Maybe this was it. I had already survived longer than I should have. I have survived a fatal knife injury, a bear attack, a killer game of chess, and Poppy's kidnapping. Maybe the heavens decided to kill me off now. Maybe they decided that I has suffered enough. Because I am suffering, I realized. I have been suffering my whole life, without realizing I had.

I shut my eyes, but something opened them. Poppy. I peeled my lips into a weak smile, as once again she saved my delicate, hanging off of a thread life. Maybe I did want to be a renowned hero, across the world. Just that thought lifted my spirit.

Clone Poppy suddenly appeared in front of me. She lent me her hand, and I took hold of it. Once again my hand stung, but I ignored the feeling. As if she were magic, the chair suddenly let go of me. I kept on holding her hand, and she helped me up gently. I hugged her, breathing the smell of her in. I remarked about the closeness of Clone Poppy's smell, and the real Poppy smell. Poppy used a rose smelling body wash, which always made her smell good. My family thought it was ironic that she was named after the flower poppy, but preferred roses' smell and look better.

 We spent two weeks in the French countryside the summer of first grade, for Poppy to see real, French poppies…

The day my dad announced we were going to France for two weeks was the day that my school got out. "Where are the top three places you want to go right now?" Dad had asked, with a grin on his face.

"I want to go to Florida, France and Costa Rica," my mother replied, smiling at him.

Poppy started to say she wanted to go to New York City and California before I interrupted her.

"I want to go to London, England and Rocky Mountain," I said as I boasted my ability to name the capital of Great Britain. In my geography class, we were learning capitals of countries that we had recently studied: France, Great Britain, United States of America, Mexico and Egypt. After many years of dumbness, I was now carving my path to a straight A student, despite the difficulties I had been through.

"Mommy, daddy, I was talking and then she," Poppy pointed her finger at me, "She intruped me. Can you put her in a timeout for ininiti?" Poppy complained, pronouncing "interrupted" and "infinity" wrong.

"Reagan, don't break the train of thought of your sister, and Poppy, don't tattle tale on Reagan," my father advised us.

We both nodded our heads, and slumped our shoulders. Both of us tried to avoid getting our parents upset, and when that did happen, we would make up as quickly as possible. Our father was a quick man to anger, and Poppy and I were always afraid of his outbursts.

My father jumped right into a good mood again, and with a cheerful, lighthearted voice, he announced to us, "How would you like to go to France in a week?" Poppy and I looked at each other, and shrugged. From the looks on our faces, we did not know what my father was saying, nor where he was going with his conversation.

"Well, we are! For two weeks! How does that sound?" Poppy's eyes widened, understanding what he said before I did.

"We get to go to Paris?" she asked, and I finally perceived what we were doing in two weeks, and where we were going: France.

"Yes, Poppy darling. We are going to the French countryside, to see all of the beautiful poppy flowers for a week, and before that we are going to Paris for a week. How does all of that sound?" my mother almost laughed. Poppy began dancing around the room, and I was seeing how much fun she was having, so I got up too and pranced around with her. We were busy doing the macarana, when I realized something.

"Poppy! We have to pack!"

"Ahhhhhhhhhhhhhhhh!"

We made a mad dash for upstairs when something grabbed at our T-shirts.

"Where are you guys going?" my dad asked, making a funny face. We laughed as he picked both of us up and swung us onto his shoulders.

"We don't leave for France for another week," my mother added, as she kissed each of our cheeks. "But now you can dream of France, little ones."

Our father carried us upstairs, breathing hard with every step. We went into Poppy's red bedroom, and dad dumped her onto her small bed the size of a sofa. He then marched into my room, and flung me on my bed. I giggled, and got up to brush my teeth.

After a week of packing, anticipation, and patience, we, the Green family left our house at 5:12am to fly to Paris France.

"France! France! France! France!" Poppy and I chanted together the whole car ride over to the nearby airport.

"Girls, can you stop, please?" our mother scolded. We stopped, but gave the other one a glance that showed how much fun we were having. The car pulled into the parking garage located at the airport, and we silently squealed.

After we parked, got our luggage and double checked for the passports, we strolled up toward the sliding glass doors that allowed us to enter the terminal.

"Remember the last time we flew on an airplane, Reagan and Poppy?" my dad asked.

"Yeah. It was long and boring," Poppy replied.

"Long and boring and a bore," I added.

We entered the long line to check out our luggage, and soon Poppy and I began complaining about how long it would take to get it all over with, even though it was almost 6:00am.

"When will we get to France? It been a google years," I grumbled.

"Reagan, we have to get through security. Then, and only then we will be able to go onto the airplane. For now we have to be patient, just like you were at the house," my mother told me, obviously getting tired of me complaining so much.

I waited in the long line, but I still was a little bored and in a bad mood. To entertain myself, I slipped off my purple jelly sandals and began to walk in circles around my parents, barefoot. Poppy perceived that I was doing this, and she slipped off her sandals. We began to dance around our parents, our bare feet pounding on the tile floor.

"Girls, stop that. There are other little girls here looking at you, and you want to set good examples, don't you?" My dad punished us. He then looked at out wiggling feet, and narrowed his eyebrows.

"Put. Your. Shoes. Back. On."

We scrambled back to our sandals, and quickly put them on, our little hearts pounding all the way to our feet.

By the time Poppy velcroed the last strap, one of the airport employees called us up, our parents walked up. We followed them, dragging our little princess suitcases and matching backpacks behind us.

"I'll take your suitcase, sweet heart," a smooth, calming voice said behind the counter that stretched all the way to the other "wall." Under the fake stone counter, there were holes big enough to fit a large suitcase, and in front of that hole was a metal plate the size of the length of the opening.

Curious, I stepped on the metal plate, but nothing happened. I jumped on it, but this time I heard the lady behind the counter say,

"Please don't do that." I stopped, and looked at my mother. She was rubbing her temples, just like the magician at my birthday party a few years before. My father was turning red, as if he were embarrassed.

We finally got through the luggage check-in, and then we traveled to the security checkpoint. Click, click, click, the shoes of the people who were around us went, so I tried to imitate them, but instead I stomped my feet. Loud.

"Stomp! Stomp! Stomp!" I yelled, pretending I was the dragon attacking the prince in my favorite princess movie. "Ahhhhh!" I dramatically fell to the floor, as if the prince had killed the dragon.

"Hey, little girl, can you, like, stop maybe? It's like, so annoying."

I looked up and a girl who looked maybe thirteen or fourteen was standing over me, her hand on her hip.

"S-S-S-sorry," I mumbled. The older girl ignored what I had just said, and snapped back at me.

"You know, little girls like you really get on my, like, nerves. Like, if I ever like, become president, I will like, ban little girls like, until they turn like, thirteen.

"Anyway, I like, have to go call Jonny, who is like, my boyfriend. I bet, like, you never, like, have a boyfriend. Toodles!" The girl sashayed away, and caught up with a group of girls around her age. They were all beautiful, and wore expensive clothing. One girl, I noticed was holding hands with a cute boy. Ewww, I thought. The girl that was picking on me positioned herself right smack in the middle of the group of six, as if she were the ruler or leader of them all. She told the group something, and they all looked back at me and laughed. I frowned at them, and reached for my mother's leg to hide behind. But it wasn't there.

"Mommy?" I called. There was no response, except a few glances in my direction. "Mommy? W-Where are you?" I called again. This time, I few more people scurrying around slowed to see who was calling. "Mommy!?" I cried. I started to sniff and my cheeks swelled up to stop the tears from falling.

"Little girl, are you O.K?" I turned around to find a woman pushing a stroller. Inside it was a baby. I walked over to the woman, her eyes flooding with worry as she kneeled down to my height.

"No. I-I can't find-d m-m-my mom-m-my." And I burst into another set of tears.

"I'll help you find her. Do you know her cell phone number?"

I nodded as she pulled out her cell phone from her pocket. She handed it to me, and I dialed my mom's number.

Ring...riiinnng...ring... "Hello? Who is this?"

"Mommy! I am with a nice lady by the security checkpoint, and I'm using her phone right now. Where are you? Where are you? Where are you?" My mouth was moving a mile per minute, for I was relieved to her my mother's voice.

"Reagan! There you are. Stay with The Nice Lady, and daddy will find you. Got that?"

"Yes, mommy."

Mom hung up the phone, and I returned it to The Nice Lady. She smiled, and so I smiled too.

"My mommy told me to stay with you until my daddy finds me. Is that O.K?" I asked her. She looked at her watch, and smiled.

"I can spare some time before Teddy and I's flight."

"Who is Teddy?"

"My son, over there in the stroller."

"He sure is cute. When I am older, I want to have a baby boy and name him Teddy. I like the name Teddy."

"Hopefully you don't have any babies for a long time."

Just as The Nice Lady said that, I heard my dad calling my name.

"Reagan! Reagan! Where are you?"

"That is my daddy. Bye bye! Thank you!"

I ran off to go find my father, and I found him at one of the small convenience stores that are always located at airports.

"Daddy! There you are!" I squealed, happy to see him. He was talking to one of the salesperson, who was looking at him with a concerned expression. She saw me, and pointed to me. Dad turned around, and relief engulfed his blue eyes. He ran over to me, and hugged me.

"There you are, Reagan. We were worried sick about you. Don't you ever do that again, do you understand? Thank God that you are alright. We were worried sick. Wait, did I just say that? I think I did, but my goodness Reagan, you really got us worried. Let's take go to mommy, how does that sound?" he jabbered.

"Daddy, I'm alright. The Nice Lady stayed with me, and she helped me find you. She also let me use her phone," I ignored my dad's gibbering and pointed to the area I stayed in with The Nice Lady. She was still there, talking on her phone. She looked upset.

"Can we go see her one last time?" I asked my father.

"It looks like she is busy. Maybe later?" he replied. I made a pouty face, and he just shook his head slowly.

"Fine. I guess I do owe The Nice Lady a thank you."

We went over to her, and she had just gotten off of the phone. By this time, she looked even more upset than she was previously.

"Are you okay?" I asked her.

"Oh... it's nothing. Did you find your daddy?"

"Yeah! He wants to talk to you."

My dad shook her hand, and introduced himself.

"I'm Nick, Reagan's dad. I just came over to say thank you.'

'It was really nothing. Reagan was such a sweet girl. I'm Jessica, by the way."

"I call you The Nice Lady, Jessica," I blurted out. The Nice Lady laughed, and started to walk away.

"I better get going. I am going to miss my flight if I don't."

"Where are you going?" my father asked The Nice Lady.

"Pittsburgh, to visit Teddy's grandfather." she replied.

"We are going to France!" I exclaimed excitedly.

"That is cool. You know, I used to live in Paris. It is a beautiful city," The Nice Lady told us.

"Did you go to college there?" my father asked her.

"No, Paris called for me, so I went."

"What was your job?" dad asked her.

"I actually worked in a little boutique called Boutique fraîche."

"We might spend a day or two in Paris, so we should go there sometime, shall we Reagan?" he asked me.

"Sure! When we go to Paris, I want to get a bracelet."

The Nice Lady only laughed, and called out to us, "Au revoir! Bon voyage!"

We then once again rushed to the security checkpoint.

"Reagan! There you are!" a voice like my mother's exclaimed. We were in line to be examined by the airport security. Then, out of the blue my mother ran up and hugged me very tight; it almost felt like she was squeezing my guts out.

"I am sorry," I apologized. Although I knew my parents were more worried about me and how I reacted when I got lost, I also knew that they would be upset after I went into details.

"Baby, how did you get lost? Was I walking too fast for you?" mom asked me.

"Well, I-I was p-pretending that I w-w-as a d-d-d-dragon, so I stop-p-ped to pretend that a-a-and I lo-ost track of you g-g-guys. I'm sorry! I'm so sorry! Please forgiv-v-ve me! Please-"

"Darling, please don't be upset. Yes, we are a bit ticked that you goofed off in a public place, but we are glad to see that you are not hurt, are okay, you knew what to do, and that you found us, mom explained to me.

We stood in the line for the security, waiting for our turn to set our backpacks in on the conveyor belt, and walk through the metal detector.

I started to yawn, so my dad picked me up and I fell right asleep on his shoulder.

"Wake up, Reagan," Poppy whispered in my ear. We were sitting in cushiony seats, which were in a row. I looked out the window that radiated light from the sun, and observed that we were a good thousand feet or so in the air as the waves of an ocean crashed beneath me.

"Are we on the airplane?" I asked curiously.

"Yes, we are," answered my mother, who sat in the aisle seat. I was in the window seat, and Poppy was in the middle.

"What time is it?" I asked.

"It is..." my mom looked at her watch on her wrist and said, "It is 12:59 back at home. Where we are now, I have no clue."

I picked up the airline magazine stored in the seat in front of me, and flipped through it. The magazine wasn't very interesting at all, for it was meant for people who had a higher reading level than I did. I sighed and put the magazine back after a couple of pages. How long is this going to take? I thought to myself.

"How much longer do we have?" I asked my mother another question.

"Reagan, be patient. We got onto the plane at seven, and it usually takes 11 hours for the flight so we have about... four to five hours left."

I groaned, and rolled my back to her. I was looking out of the window when I spotted something underneath us. Was it land? Could it be? I closed my eyes, and opened them again. There it was again! And then it disappeared. Dang it. Wait a minute, there it was! Green and vibrant grass, I saw sheep below, eating it. There were cows, and trees and small, little cottages.

"Poppy! Look! Land! I see land! I see land! There is land right out of the window right now! Come see, Poppy. Come see the glorious, green land! Do you think that we are in France? Do you? Mommy! I see land! Mommy, look! Look now! Where is daddy? Can I tell him that I see-"

"Pleez be quiet, chaild. We see da land and know it is dere, so please sooth ur loud, big fat mouth," snapped an old, gross man in the seat in front of me.

"Sorry, sir. She gets a little...a little wound up and excited," my mother apologized.

"Yeah, I'm sorry old man. I was excited to see the sheep, and the little tiny houses below me. I won't do it again. I promise. Cross my heart, I promise I won't do it again," I also apologize trying to act like my mother.

"Well, I don't care whut ya gonna do as long as ya shut ur yap."

My mother smiled in an embarrassed way, and frowned when she turned to me.

"Reagan, you have got to keep your noise level limited. Everything you say, everything you do is loud, and embarrassing," she yelled at me, but in reality she whisper/yelled at the same time.

"I truly am sorry, mommy. Sometimes I get excited, and start to be loud," I sniffed. My mother only shook her head, and looked at her phone.

"Vous voulez manger quelque chose, Mademoiselle?" a voice said.

"Excuse me?" I said, as if she were speaking another language, which she was. French, to be exact.

"Would you like anything, Miss?" the woman was a flight attendant, who wore a blue skirt, a matching blue blouse, and a white dress coat with a pin on it that read Clara Martin. Her

black hair was tied up in a neat bun, and she had a heavy French accent.

"Could I please get a cranberry juice, please?" I asked her, as polite as I could be.

"Oui. And for the little girl in the middle row?"

I looked at Poppy, and said the drink she absolutely loved. Orange juice.

"Oh, she will have orange juice in a princess cup. Please."

"And for your mama?"

"Water, please."

The flight attendant smiled, and walked to the row behind me. I heard her speak French, but this time the people behind us understood her.

"Bonjour, aimeriez-vous des Articles de notre menu?" she asked the row.

"Puis-je avoir de l'eau avec de la glace? Je vous remercie."

"Oui. Ce sera tout? "

"Une dernière chose, pourrais-je avoir encore une eau pour Marie?"

"Aucun problème. Autre chose que tu veux?"

"Merci mademoiselle. Au revoir."

She then moved to the row after, and they too spoke fluent French.

"Poppy," I whispered to her, "She speaks French."

Poppy opened her eyes, slowly since she had been sleeping.

"Cool," she whispered and fell back asleep.

"Mesdames et Messieurs, veuillez attacher votre ceinture et préparez-vous à atterrir. Merci d'avoir choisi les compagnies aériennes américaines françaises, et bonne journée." I jolted myself awake as the overhead speaker blasted both French, and English.

"Ladies and gentlemen, please fasten your seatbelts and prepare for landing. Thank you for choosing French American Airlines, and have a nice day."

The ground came closer and closer, and I grew more and more excited for the next few weeks. The airport became visible, and I was in awe of the modern, sleek look it gave off.

"Mommy! Look!" I excitedly yelled at her.

"Cool, sweetie."

I watched as the plane came closer and closer to the ground, and as the space between the ground and the place became smaller and smaller.

"5...4..." I counted down, quietly. "...3...2...1." the plane touched the runway, and jerked me backward in my seat.

"Bienvenue à Paris, France. French American Airlines espérait que vous ayez un vol confortable. merci de voler avec nous, et nous espérons vous voir prochainement," the overhead speaker told us.

"Welcome to Paris, France. French American Airlines hopes you had a comfortable flight. Thank you for flying with us, and we hope that we will see you soon."

"Ummm... pourriez-vous s'il vous plaît nous emmener à l'Hôtel Kings, monsieur?" my mother asked our taxi driver in a really bad French accent.

"Madem, zhat vwill be avound vivteen U.S dollars," the taxi driver said, as if he delt with bad speaking Americans all of the time.

We drove in silence, but every once in awhile we would see a well known monument, like the

Eiffel Tower or Arc de Triomphe, and gasp in amazement.

The car eventually stopped, and I looked out of the window. There stood our hotel, which was made of stone and brick. It was small, with only a few small windows peeping out from all of the brick and glimmering white stone.

We got all of the luggage from the taxi, payed the grumpy driver, and walked into the cozy hotel.

The lobby was decorated as if it were a small living room itself. The wood floor was a welcoming brown color, and the furniture was all a yellow; the sofa, the chairs. Even the rug was a soft yellow color.

"Bonjour, comment puis-je vous aider, madame?" Said a hotel clerk behind the yellow counter.

"Um, nous avons réservé une chambre d'hôtel, et nous aimerions vérifier à ce moment-là," my mother said once again in a really bad French accent.

"Voici votre clé, madame." The hotel clerk sighed, and handed her a room key. He mumbled something in French, and showed us

to the one, tiny elevator that could only fit two people and a suitcase.

"I'll ride on it, and bring all of the suitcases up," my father offered.

"Perfect," my mother said. "And I will stay down here to watch the suitcases."

After a few trips up and down the elevator, my parents successfully transported all of the luggage to the second floor, where we would be staying. "Let's see our room," my mother announced once all of us were up with the luggage. (Poppy and I had to stay on the ground floor to watch the luggage that was there.) My mother unlocked the door, and we walked into a room with two bed, a small TV that looked as it would break, and one little desk. There was a toilet and sink, with the smallest shower I had ever seen. Just like the lobby, everything was yellow. The walls, the quilts on the beds, the lampshade, even the toilet was yellow. The same, soft boring yellow. The only thing that was not yellow was the carpet, which was a soft brown, like the wood floors in the lobby.

"This is... interesting," my father said, looking around. The small window gave little light in the room, so we all had to squint hard. And as is if

the small window weren't enough, the lamp's light bulb was burnt out.

We all sat on the beds, and relaxed from the long travel day.

"Let's go see Paris!" wailed my sister, who was already dressed in a red dress with little pink roses printed on the sleeves. I groaned, and slowly sat up and looked around. My parents were also dressed.

"Come on, Reagan. We are going to the Eiffel Tower, and I don't think that you'd want to miss it," my mother advised me.

I slid out of the bed, onto the carpet and like a tortoise, I shuffled over to my suitcase. I picked out my ink dress with the collar, and changed into it.

"We are going to the Eiffel Tower! We are going to the Eiffel Tower!" Poppy and I chanted as loud as we could. We were walking in the streets of the historical city, and admiring all of the boutiques and patisseries with the delicious looking bread and pastries.

"Can we get one?" I asked my parents, who shook their heads no.

The French people biking next to us smiled as Poppy and I kept chanting our little song. It felt good to be noticed, especially since I did not have any friends at the time.

"Bonjour," a girl about my age said to me as she passed by, probably headed to school.

"Bunjoor?" I tried, knowing that I was like my mother, who couldn't pronounce anything right.

"Mommy, what does Bunjoor mean in France?" I asked my mother

"It means hello, Reagan."

We walked on, occasionally stopping into stores, and looking at all of the treasures.

"I love this," Poppy said to me, holding up a violet bow that was in a small boutique near the Eiffel Tower.

"That is cool," I said. I imagined all of the girls being jealous of me since they did not have any French bows, especially from Paris. Well, maybe Sassy Berg had one. She was rich, so her parents gave her everything she wanted.

"Where did you find those?" I asked Poppy. She pointed to a small corner by the entrance to the boutique.

"Thanks," and I dashed over to the corner.

Blue, green, hot pink, purple, turquoise, yellow. All of the bows had their own color, and I picked up the hot pink one.

"Mommy?'" I called, but she did not answer. "Mommy?"

"Right over here. We are going to go soon, sweetie," she answered to my call.

I carefully put the bow back, and blew it a kiss.

"Bienvenue à la Tour Eiffel. Cette belle structure a été construite de 1897 à 1889 par Gustave Eiffel pour l'exposition universelle," the tour guide said to us in both English and France.

"Welcome to ze Eiffel Tower. Sis beautiful structer was built en 1887 and it vas winished in 1889. Gustav Eiffel consroocteed zis for World Faire, Viche was en also 1889."

The tower loomed in front of us, the iron twisting into a masterpiece that everyone knew.

"Zis tower has overe zeven milloone visitors a year."

The tour then moved to the bank of elevators, and they soared up a viewing floor.

"Mommy! Daddy! Look at the awesome view!" I exclaimed.

The seine river streamed below, as the city of light bustle beneath. Church bells rang and echoed across Paris, and fountains burbled. The wind slightly swayed the tower, and I griped my mother's leg.

"Okay, time's oop," the tour guide said to us. We traveled down the elevators, and the other guide handed us brochures about the tower, but mine was in French.

"La tour Eiffel!" Mine said. I opened it up, and all I looked at were the pictures of the founder, the building process, and the tower today.

"This brochure is boring," I complained, and dumped the brochure in the trash can by the entrance to the Eiffel Tower.

"Let's stop for lunch since it is 12:20," my mother suggested after we were back walking to our hotel.

"Can we go there?" I asked, pointing to a small restaurant called "La cachette du cuisinier."

My parents nodded, and we walked into the restaurant.

"Bonjour, une table pour quatre?" a waitress asked us.

"Pardonnez-moi, mais parlez-vous anglais?" my mother asked her, flipping the pages of her French-to-English handbook.

"Yes, madam. Would yo like ay tabeel for four?"

The week of Paris was basically like that the whole time. We rented a car to go to Gourdes, a very charming French Town with winding streets, and a peaceful vibe.

"Let's go to the poppies now!" Poppy urged. It was our fourth day in Gourdes, and every day, Poppy would ask us that same old question over. And over. And over. And over.

"Everyone get in the car!" my mother called, for my father was putting stuff in the safe provided in the hotel room.

"Yes! Poppies, get ready because here Poppy comes!" Poppy jumped on the bed. We all laughed and took the elevator to the glamorous lobby.

"Come on. You guys are sooooo slow," Poppy complained. A whoosh of warm, spring air welcomed us as we opened the heavy door that led us to the parking lot, where the rental car

was parked. All of us got in, and backed out of the space.

"Are we there yet? Are we there yet? Are we there yet?" Poppy asked me.

"Poppy, we have only driven for ten minutes, so it will take us another hour or so," mom responded to her. Buildings passed by us as we drove to the poppy fields. I had fun waving at all of the people I saw walking on the stone sidewalks.

"It sure is a beautiful city," my mother said to us. My father nodded and turned on his blinked. I closed my eyes, for I was tired. Poppy had been continuously waking me the last night, telling me how excited she was about seeing all of the fields of poppies. I then fell into a deep sleep, and did not wake until we arrived at the Poppy fields.

"Let's take a picture, and then scurry off. We are not supposed to be doing this, since this isn't our property," my father explained. Poppy ignored him, opened the car door and started sprinting toward the beautiful field of poppies, which were all red.

My father pulled out his camera, and urged me to go with her. I smiled and ran out to join the fun. The flowers tickled my ankles as I cautiously ran to Poppy, for I tried not to smash the delicate petals.

"Tag, you're it!" Poppy announced, touching my shoulder, and quickly pulling her hand back. She dashed off, twisting her body in ways I never could. I sprinted for her, my feet pounding on the soft poppies. I barely managed to grab her hair, when my father called for us.

"Time to go, girls!" he started to walk across the sea of red poppies.

"Race you," I whispered to Poppy. She nodded, and began to count down from ten.

"Ten...nine...seven..." I joined the totally wrong countdown, and prepared to shoot off like a bullet.

"Three... two... one... GO!" we dashed off, legs moving, arms pumping. I breathed hard for almost no air, but kept pushing myself faster, and faster, to the point when I was about to collapse. I closed my eyes, trying to ease the pain, but it did not get any better.

Go, I urged myself. Faster, faster, I opened my eyes. Poppy was parallel to me.

I eventually gave up, only two feet from the finish line.

"I won!" Poppy celebrated her defeat while I looked out of the car window, watching the fields of lavender and poppies.

"Poppy, let's not brag. Did you like the field of poppies?" my father asked her.

"The poppies were okay. I like roses much better," she replied. The car burst in a round of laughter, and it didn't stop until we got home.

Clone Poppy led me out of the shack, and disappeared into thin air. Once again, I was alone in the maze. I sighed, and started moving my sore legs in the direction I was going before I was interrupted by the hissing sound. I felt my back for my backpack, but it wasn't there, and when I turned around, the shack wasn't where it was.

It was gone.

Chapter 23- Souls

Wake up, I slowly eased myself after a night of rest. The sun was rising, and I reached out for my backpack to check the time, and eat something.

Oh. Right. The stupid shack disappeared, with all of my food, water, and clothing, and Nilly's cell phone.

I stood up, and began to walk again. My burnt back felt a little better, but not much. I heard a strange shuffling noise, and looked behind me. No one was there.

"Hello?" I called out, but I knew doing that was useless. Whatever was behind me knew my exact location, if it did not already. Again, I looked behind me after the sound grew nearer.

Not the chess game again, I complained to myself.

My heart began to race, for when I turned a corner I spotted a black figure, who was almost entirely transparent. He began to howl, and more and more of them appeared, howling and screaming. I began to run, as my palms sweat. They howled words, it seemed.

"Souls. Free. Souls. Free," they chanted to me in an echoing, haunting voice that turned into chills as they ran down my back.

I ran, twisting and turning throughout the maze. I could feel in my bones that I was getting closer to Poppy. I turned a right, and another right.

"Run," I urged myself. "Run like you did in with Poppy in the poppy field that day."

I stopped, and turned around. The souls quickly disappeared in the walls of Dolor Aegritudo In Ocul Familia De La Grene, but I could still feel them watching me. Their beady, empty eyes watching me like a hawk. It was only one step I took when they came out.

The souls attacked me, as if I was only but a small mouse. But I wasn't. I tried to grab hold of them, but my hand passed through their skin. As I did this, in the corner of my eye I saw a soul raise a transparent sickle, and it came down.

The world went black.

"Get off," I murmured as I twisted myself to get them off. I was half asleep, and I instantly woke up when I remembered where I was, and what was happening to me. I stood up, and the souls all fell off, one by one, and dissolved into the gravestones. It seemed as if the stones were their own gravestones; they died and were buried. A soul dressed in a satin dress dissolved into a gravestone that read Alyssa Mickle, December 5, 1895- June 6, 1944.

I looked around, and just behind me stood a silver cage, with Poppy in it. She was wearing a white dress with blood stains on it, and her hair was in a bun, with silver decals. Photos were scattered across the floor of the gleaming silver cage, and I noticed that they were photos of me and our broken family.

"Poppy! There you are! Let me get you out! Come! Please!" I exclaimed, while a tear trickled down her pale face.

"Go. Run. Leave me, Reagan. This is a trap, just to kill you," she whispered in a hoarse voice, as if she hadn't been eating or drinking for the few days she had been kidnapped.

"But I can't leave you," I told her, my happy voice fading into a sad one, like Poppy's.

"You have to. Go. Don't come back, never come back. Never."

"Please, Poppy, come with me. Ms. Grande will take care of us, and-"

"No. Go, now before they kill you." I slowly went away, and turned away from her. I then ran, tearing at my clothing when all of the sudden I was in a field of bright red poppies, like the ones in France.

"Oh no," I whispered to myself. I walked slowly across the field, heart pounding and hands sweating. It smelled too sweet.

The poppies started releasing a gas out of their petals, just like the gas I inhaled at the hospital, except this gas was deadly, and my parents created it. I twisted my head, looking for shelter. Behind me was an old colonial house that creaked in the slight, mysterious breeze. I sprinted toward it, but I tripped on a small stick. I scurried to get up, but at this point I was too weak. I laid there, and I heard someone, I lifted my head up, and saw Clone Poppy.

"Come on, Reagan. You found her already, and can find her again," she coaxed me. I took her hand, which she held out to me.

"Ouch." this time, there was more pain when I touched her, and the glass left a slight rash.

Clone Poppy helped me to the colonial house, and opened the door. The entrance to the maze was on the other side of it, and I walked towards it.

Once again, the red curtain swayed in the wind, taunting me. I coughed, trying to get the gas out of my lungs. My throat hurt by the time I stopped coughing, and I entered Dolor Aegritudo In Ocul Familia De La Grene again.

Click. Click. Click. Even though my shoes were worn from walking so much, they still clicked against the gravestones. This time my mission was not to only find Poppy and kill my parents, but to survive. I tied my long, blonde hair in a high ponytail, and double knotted my shoe laces.

"Mommy, daddy, here I come," I shouted into the maze, trying to intimidate them, but I probably wasn't to them. To my parents, I was a little girl who had dreams bigger than herself. A little girl that was a waste of time; a little girl that was useless. But I would show them...

I just had to find Poppy first.

"Black socks they never get dirty the longer you wear them the stronger they get, sometimes I think I should wash them but something keeps telling me don't wash them yet... not yet... not... yet," I sang, trying to distract myself from my hunger. Eventually, I started to cry. I was hungry, tired, thirsty, and in pain. My sister was kidnapped, my best friend was killed, and my parents were criminals. The tears rolled down my red cheeks, sobbing and singing at the same time.

The maze seemed longer than the first time I had gone through. My steps became shorter and shorter, as my eyelids grew more and more heavy. I felt as if I were a living zombie.

"Tweet. Tweet." The soft singing of a bird. I looked around, trying to catch a glimpse of the little creature, but with my double vision it was hard for me too.

"Tweet tweet tweet," it sang, but this time the small little tune became a little less sweet and merry as it was before. I smelled a familiar scent. Fish, like the time at Fishin' Larry's Fish and Bar. I was six or seven, and my parents won a trip for four to Florida. We stopped by a fish restaurant at the airport after a long day of traveling, and I ordered salmon with lemon zest. It was my first time having fish, and I hated it. The fish I smelled now smelled like the ocean, instead of lemon.

I spotted the little bird on top of one of the maze's walls. He was an ivory color, and looked like a dove. But as soon as I noticed him, he transformed into a seagull, who squawked at me.

That's funny, I thought. You usually don't see seagulls in Colorado. I started hearing waves crashing, like at a beach. I started to run, and after a few minutes of doing so I witnessed a big wall of water coming straight towards me.

Chapter 24- Oscar

I started running as fast as I could, but it was hard to breath. I could feel the water coming fast, so that meant I had to run fast. If not, faster than fast. I felt the water touching my ankles, and then I was washed up in it. The waves dunked my head under over and over and over again. The only air I got was the short breaths when the waves allowed me to swim to the surface, and still I was suffocating.

The water was cold, like ice and it was hard to move in. I took swimming lessons for a year, and then quit. I only had a tiny knowledge of how to save myself in a situation like this, since my swim instructor spent more time on telling me how to instead of showing me.

My arms flung around, hoping someone would see, but I knew nobody would. I was all alone, and the only people watching me drown were my parents, and possibly Clone Poppy.

My sore, useless legs kicked as hard as they could to keep my head above the surface. Not that being above the surface would help. My lungs were panicked and trying to breath heavy, but I was only choking on water.

"Help!" I gasped, praying that somebody would hear me. Not that they would, but I felt better getting all of my sadness, anger and frustration with the world out by screaming and crying. "Help. Me!" I gasped, knowing that if I wasn't rescued in a few minutes, I would be gone from this spinning globe.

I felt myself swirling, just a little bit, and then sinking. Going down, down. The current dragged me like I was a teddy bear that belonged to a six year old. I tried to beat the rushing water, but I couldn't. It was too strong for my weak bones. I was tugged down even deeper, until my ears started popping like they were fireworks. The air I had been storing in my lungs was now drifting up to the surface, for I was too weak to hold it in much longer. The current forced me to the ground of the maze, and I laid with the gravestones. I watched as the very last air in my lungs drifted up, swirling and fighting the other bubbles. I looked around me, and there were the undead souls, relaxing like this was normal, to be pinned to the ground while water crashed above you. They smiled and waved at me, as if I were to join their little party: killing people, and haunting the maze.

With the last energy I had, I pushed off the bottom of the maze, and kicked up to the surface, where I had my fullest breath I had ever had. I swam to where the water abruptly stopped, and let myself fall 20 feet to the damp grass and gravestones. I laid there, gulping air and recovering from the long, hard fall.

I stumbled up, with a migraine and blurry vision. I moaned, and toppled over as if I were a domino. I opened my eyes to find a figure standing in front of me, and then fell into a deep, dark sleep.

"Are you okay?" a voice asked me. It was young, not mature like a teenager's or adult's.

I opened my eyes, and I was in a wooden hut. From what I could tell, it was still in the maze, but we were safer.

"Who a-a-are you?" I asked him.

"I'm...I'm Oscar," he replied with a smile. He had red hair, freckles, and a toothy smile. His British accent made me calmer about him. Like Poppy was, he was dressed in simple white. A white dress shirt with silver buttons, white overalls and a white cap that was monogrammed with the numbers 3764.

"I'm Reagan. How did you end up in the maze?" I asked Oscar.

"I was captured by a...by a psycho husband and wife, and they put me... they put me in a silver cage, you see. I escaped... well not really escaped but anyway... I escaped since I grew so skinny... because I wasn't... I wasn't eating enough. They let me go, but... they let me go but on one circumstance: I am...I am never ever allowed...never allowed to leave the... the maze," he explained to me.

"Why did they kidnap you?"

"You see, my family is...very rich, and the couple came to rob our house. They threatened to take away my sister, Valerie, who is my father's... favorite, and unfortunately he told them to take me... instead. Probably... probably because I accidentally caught the East... Wing on fire but that is a whole... another story that you don't want to... hear."

"Cool."

"Why are you here?"

"My sister was taken by my parents and-"

"Those people... are your... parents?!"

"Yeah... back on topic, they left me little notes that led me to the maze and so here I am."

"Oh. That is… interesting? I don't know. Sometimes I don't know what to say… it's a genetic disorder that my mother has. I apologize in advance … in advance for saying things I may not mean," Oscar murmured, as if he were embarrassed.

"No it's fine," I reassured him. "In fact, I think my great great great aunt had a reading thingy. I'm not going to judge you."

"Thanks. In my family, we believe that a disorder… like mine… is a thing to be… ashamed about…"

"If that is the case, then consider me your family. I'll gladly be your friend. Unless you don't want to be," I offered.

"Yes, I will be. And can I… make a… suggestion?"

"Sure."

"Can I help… you find your… sister?"

My mouth twisted its way into a smile, and I hugged Oscar.

"Thank you so much! This is my second time in the maze, and I need help! Thank you! Thank you!"

"No... problem. It... it feels good... to know the people... you love are... they are safe."

Oscar turned his back to me, looking for something. He pulled out a small fruit, on that I had never seen before. It was yellow, with little dots of a faint green. The fruit was shaped like an oval. It had little spikes on the outside, and it was very fragrant. The yellow fruit smelled like a refreshing mint, with a trace of strawberry scent.

"What the heck is that?" I asked him, eyeing the strange item.

"It is a...Mûrirlaplaie. It only grows... in the maze. Apparently, your parents... created their own berry, so... they could live."

"Wait, where do they live? They can't possibly live in the maze, can they?"

"Yeah, they live in... they live in the maze alright."

"Where in the maze?"

"The maze... it is their... house, so technically...you are trespassing. We... we are trespassing. They can literally... they can control the maze themselves... with a... with... dang. I forgot."

I sighed. I had hoped that I could figure out where they were at the very minute, and how they were controlling the maze.

"Thanks anyways. And I have a question, um, how come there were no dead ends when I went through the maze?"

"Your...parents built this maze for not only you and your sister. I have been here over four years. Dolor Aegritudo In Ocul Familia De La Grene has...it has been operating for over ten years. They tell all of the inmates...the story...of how they... of how they became...evil and yadda yadda yadda."

"Can you possibly tell me the story?"

Oscar sighed, and cleared his throat.

"Well... okay. Basically a cousin... a cousin flushed... a cousin flushed your mom's jewelry down the... the... the toilet... and she turned... what is that word...evil."

"But, I was the one who flushed the jewelry down the toilet. Why did my mother lie? I don't have any cousins."

"Wait... you can...you where...were the person that flushed the stuff...flushed it down the toilet?"

"Yeah," I blushed.

Oscar handed me a Mûrirlaplaie, and I bit into it. It was sweet, like sugar and had a little bit of a tang, like a lemony flavor.

"This is good!" I exclaimed, with bits of the fruit stuck in between my teeth, since it was chewy.

"Yeah. if you look under the gravestones, there is... there is at least... at least three or four of the Mûrirlaplaie... that's what another prisoner told me... and-"

"There are more prisoners? I need to fix this."

"There...is no way."

"Why? How?"

"Reagan, your parents found a way to make themselves indestructible, but the maze can kill them. That is the only way to do so. One of the prisoners snuck a gun into the maze, and... and they tried... tried to... they tried to kill them. It did not work, and... and the bullets... they ricocheted off of their bodies. I saw it with my own... with my own eyes."

"What did they do to the-to him?"

"The bullet shot back into his cage... and it... and it killed... it killed him."

"What was his name?"

"Juli...Julius."

"Oh."

We sat in silence as I was mourning the many murder victims of my parents. I then realized that we would never be a real family again; if they ever went to jail, they would be charged from murder, to shoplifting. They would probably earn a spot in jail for a long time. My guess was up to 90 years in a cell. I would have to be alive for 90 more years, and I would have my own family. I would have my own children, my own husband, even grandchildren and possibly great grandchildren. My mom and dad would never survive, since they were in their forties then.

Boy was this one mental rollercoaster.

Chapter 25- Sketch

"Good... good morning," Oscar chirped with a grin, waking me up from a long night's rest. He had dark circles under his eyes, and he was pale.

"Good morning Oscar." I was sleeping on a cot made of grass in his little shack made of sticks. I looked around, feeling a warmth I hadn't felt in a while. I felt safe, and I felt at home. The little shack was only about five feet across, and three feet in height. For Oscar, he could crawl easily around the shack while I stood at six foot on my very tip-toes. The only decor in the small area was a sketch of six people hung up on a stick with the sap of a maple tree. I thought it was Oscar and his family, but I could tell from the way he talked about them last he was sensitive on the subject.

"I was up all...all night thinking," Oscar started talking, so I directed my attention to him. "I was thinking how... I was thinking how we...how we could defeat your parents. When I was... when I was a prisoner to them... they seemed... they seemed to be afraid of... afraid of...mirrors."

"How? Why? I knew we had mirrors in my ho- well, maybe we did not!"

"Yeah... yeah a girl... she had a... had a pocket mirror... a mirror when I... when I first got here... and... your parents... they began... screaming and... screaming and crying... so they asked her to... they asked her to put it... to put the mirror away. And when she... when she refused... they... they... they murdered... they murdered her... in front of... in front of all of us."

I nodded understandingly. Now that I knew what they really did, I wasn't surprised that they were slowly killing off children, one by one.

"Now that we know what they are...are afraid of, what do we do now? We can't just leave all of these children to die and live their lives in a silver cage. I say we pursue them- the prisoners to have revolt," I whispered to Oscar.

"No. Even... even more people will... they will be slaughtered. We... we need to bring the walls of the maze...the walls of the maze down, that will... that will ensure we...we kill them," he whispered back.

"But that will also kill everyone in the maze, too. Do we want to kill dozens of innocent people for two outlaws? We would risk our own lives, too. And anyway, how would we destroy the maze?"

"I don't...I don't know. But I...but I will tell... I will tell you, it has its own... its own... own weakness."

"How will we figure out what its weaknesses are?"

Oscar only shook his head. And then looked at me.

"We... we will ask the... ask the animarum. They will surely have an answer for us... have an answer for us... since we... since they were created... created by your... your parents created them."

"Who are the animarum?"

"They... they are the souls... that attack... that attacked you."

"How do you know they attacked me?"

"I... I was there... I was there that day."

"How? There was nobody around me."

"If... if you... if you look closely... there... there are cameras everywhere. I hacked... I hacked them, so... so I could see what... what was going on... and I was looking... I was looking at where they usually attack... people... where they usually attack people... and sighted you. I... I tried to... I tried to rush to your aid... and then they... the animarum... the animarum attacked me, also."

"Oh. I thought- never mind."

"I'm going to go... I'm going to go get... go get breakfast."

Oscar crawled out of the shack, leaving me alone. I moved myself over to look at the sketch again, the one with his family. I stared at it, mesmerized with the detail and perfection of the artist's strokes. The figure that stood out to me the most was a girl, you looked around sixteen. She was decorated in jewelry and nicer clothing than the others, and what I would assume as Oscar's father looked down at her, beaming in pride.

That must be Valerie, I thought to myself. Next to her was Oscar, who was only half smiling. On the right of him was his mother, who was holding a little baby girl with a golden necklace around her little neck with the initials ADK. There were two more people, but they were both older than Oscar. One was a boy, and the other was a girl.

"What... what are you... you doing?" Oscar was behind me, with a handful of Mûrirlaplaie.

"I was looking at the sketch. It is really good. Whoever drew this is a really good artist.

"I... I drew it. Please, step... step away from... away from the sketch."

"Why?"

"Just... just do it... do it please?"

"Okay."

I stepped away from the sketch, and asked Oscar, "Why is the sketch so important

to you?"

"No... no reason."

We sat in an awkward silence for about ten minutes, and then I heard a crunching noise. I looked out of the little opening that led out of the shack, and spotted a human foot dressed with dark black loafers.

"Hello," I called, my heart pounding. I crawled out, and a man in a dark coat raised a little charm shaped like a black eye with his black glove, and I fell into a deep, dark sleep.

```
Chapter 26- Blind
```

"Reagan! Reagan! Wake... wake up. Wake up!" I stirred, and moaned. I opened my eyes, which were sore, and saw nothing.

"I can't see," I murmured, ignoring Oscar's cries. I opened and shut my eyes again, hoping that I would see, but I couldn't. "I can't see! Help me, Oscar, please! Help me, I can't see!"

"How... how many... many fingers... how many fingers... are...am I holding up?" He asked, and I could feel how nervous he was

"Zero? I can't see."

"I... I think... I think that you... that you are blind... you are blind."

"What?!"

"I think that you... that you-"

"You think I'm Blind."

"Yes."

Once more, I began to panic. My heartbeat quickened its pace. I had lost my vision, forever. Everything I saw, everything I did, every move I made relied on my vision. I would never see Poppy again. I would never see any of my belongings, not anything ever again. I might as well died, because it sure felt like I had. Tears began to fall, and my fingers began to shake. My hands searched for Oscar, but I couldn't find him.

"Oscar!" I cried.

"Reagan, I'm here."

My hands searched in the direction that Oscar's soothing voice came in, but yet again I found nothing. I pulled my shaking hands back, and decided to talk to Oscar about something else.

"How sniff are we going to find my sniff parents? We don't sniff know if they are out kidnapping sniff even more sniff children now."

"They... they only...kidnap people on Tuesdays."

"Why? Oh. Now that I think of it Poppy was kidnapped on a Tuesday."

"And it is... it it... is Friday... right now."

"Great! I say that we launch our attack on them now."

"No. We... we need to attack the wall of the maze... attack the maze and...and so we...so we can kill everybody...everybody inside it."

"Then let's do it today."

"We need...we need a plan... a plan first. That... that will take... that will take us... a few day...a few days."

"Then let's start to plan now."

Although my sightless eyes distracted me, we managed to come up with a good plan: Oscar discovered, when thrown on the ground, that the Mûrirlaplaie were explosive. He told me the story when he had first gotten out of the silver cage, he had found out about the fruit. He was too feeble to hold it, and it dropped to the ground. Although the explosion was not big, it had startled poor Oscar and made him realize that one day, it could be used as a weapon. "Let's... lets... make sure they still are explosive."

I nodded, and walked outside with him, linking arms because in my head, it was too risky for me to walk outside and run into a wall. My one arm was in front of me, just in case I would run into anything. Which I didn't. I heard him as he let go of the fruit, and it hitting the grass. Boom!

"It surely still... it surely still works nicely."

After we were reassured about our weapon choice, he worked with me on how to fight without any vision. For hours and hours, we worked on many moves and how to defend myself if there was ever an attack until I mastered each and every one of them and memorized the sounds of a punch, kick, even knives being flung at me by people. I learned how to climb the maze's rough stone walls, and how to drop Mûrirlaplaie down below. We estimated that if we dropped ten of them all together, that would be enough to at least damage a little bit of the maze. Oscar, being an engineering genius, pointed out several places that had flaws. These were the places we would attack, we decided.

After staying up the whole night, we had ourselves a solid plan. Of course, neither of us knew it it would work or not, but either way we would have at least tried. We could die trying, but we would've died for a good reason.

"Time to go," Oscar announced. We had been spending all morning and night gathering Mûrirlaplaie, and estimated we had about one hundred or so. About ten blows, if we used them right and at the right places. Together, we went over our plan one last time, and we went our separate ways.

"Good luck," I said to Oscar. This was probably going to be the last time that I would see him, and I gave him a brief hug.

"Be careful," he returned my wishes.

I began to climb the walls, carrying the bombs in my red sweatshirt, which was tied around my waist like it was a fanny pack. I pulled myself up the stones, one by one like I was in PE doing the annual rock climbing thing. I finally reached the top, and as I did I met a slight breeze. I knew it didn't feel so strong now, but the more and more I worked myself, the stronger and stronger it felt. I crawled on the top of the ginormous walls, which were only about three or four feet wide.

My fingers skimmed for cracks in the smooth stone. The actual wall that I had climbed was made out of stone, just like the stonework you would see in a house. The top of the wall was smooth, so rain and snow would move off easier.

After about two or three hours, my fingers felt a wide crack in the stone. It had to be at least one or two inches thick, so this meant the dirt it was resting on was too soft, so it was not very stable. I counted ten of the Mûrirlaplaie, and dropped them all at once, creating an explosion.

The wall in the area began to crumble, and I crawled away as fast as I could. I could hear miles and miles of the maze crashing down, and I scurried to find the next imperfection in the maze.

One after one, I dropped the Mûrirlaplaie, crumbling the maze into ruins. Voices became more and closer, until I could hear what they say, even from twenty feet above them. "I am hungry." "I want my mom and dad!" "Will anyone ever rescue us?" I felt bad for them.

I kept on crawling, ignoring the children's voices. The smooth stone started to slope at an angle, and I began to slide down. My fingernails dug into the slick surface, but I couldn't hold on any longer. I let go, falling through the smoky air. I landed on the ground, breathing hard. My legs hurt, probably because I landed on them.

"Woah! Reagan... are you... are you okay? That... that was quite... was quite a...a fall."

I could feel Oscar leaning over me, examining my condition.

"Oscar! I have about ten Mûrirlaplaie left. I was thinking we could lure my parents to foundation flaw etc., and we could be on top of the maze, so we can really drop bombs below."

"That sounds fine, although I'm going…. I'm going to… to…. to gather more… more weapons. I was… I was thinking that we… that we could drop… that we could drop… thirty or forty at anime…sorry, at a time… so it would be very… very strong."

I heard Oscar walk off, and lift up gravestones. Snap. "I got four… I have four, Reagan," He said, with pride. I then heard him shuffle himself over to the next stone, and pick Mûrirlaplaie. Snap, snap. "I got five!"

The farther and farther Oscar went, I followed him.

Snap. "Here are three," and he handed the fruit to me. I put them in my make-do fanny pack, and I added the next bundle that Oscar gave me.

"I think we have thirty, now," I called to him, since Oscar was a distance away from me.

"Okay… okay, I think… I think that… that… that we could… we could get ten more… ten more, and we… we could really… I think that we could totally… totally destroy the maze."

Oscar dumped the last bundle into my arms, since my fanny pack was full. We went over our new and improved plan, and we walked together, slowly.

"Where would you think my parents would be? With the prisoners? At the beginning of the maze?" I asked Oscar, since he knew his way around the maze.

"I... I would think... think that they are... that they are with the prisoners."

I nodded, and followed the sound of Oscar's silent footsteps. We walked together for at least an hour.

"Here we are."

I could feel the tension in the thick air, along with the sorrow, and the anger that lingered.

"Who are they?" "Are they prisoners?" "Why is she carrying fruit?" I heard all of them asking from their own silver cages.

"Where are the... the... Greens?" Oscar demanded.

"I last saw them at the "F" section," a girl with a sweet voice replied.

"Thanks..." I heard Oscar say, but it was much tenser than his usual voice.

"Are you okay? And what is the "F" section?" I asked him.

"Yeah, I'm fine," he started after we were out of earshot of the prisoners. "The "F" section... you know... you know how sometimes you are randomly assigned... assigned groups of... groups of people that...you don't want to be with? Well... I was assigned that group. When... when you first... when I first came in.... in the maze, I was... we are ranked... ranked by size.... size and strength, and... and family... yeah, family... I... I think. And you are... you are ranked from... from a scale of one... one to ten. For... for size... for size I was only... I was only ranked a six out of ten, for... for strength, only a four...only a four out of ten... and a... nine out... nine out of... ten for... for the family... for the family category. I... was put... I was put in the "F" group, which is the worst. They starve you, and make you work of building the maze. So... that is why I wanted... why I wanted to kill... wanted to kill the kids in...In my group since... since they were... they were bullies to me."

He was now guiding me through the maze, taking left and right turns.

"Stop messing around, 6367! Now because of your behavior, you all will have an extra hour of labor." Oh no. That was my father's voice.

```
Chapter 27- Our Own Little
Battles
```

"I think that we should start climbing now," Oscar said. I nodded, and heaved myself up the wall, one step at a time. I could feel one of the Mûrirlaplaie slip out of my arms, and made a boom that echoed itself all around the maze below. "Oops," I said to myself. I reached the top of the maze's wall, and I turned my ears downward so I could hear what was going on. I heard Oscar climbing the wall, and that was it. I blew the breath I had been holding out, and I crawled out of Oscar's general direction.

"Okay, let's crawl over to where your parents are, and let... and let's just... just drop them," he said, referring to the Mûrirlaplaie. I nodded, and we crawled closer and closer to the voices of my father and mother, who was also punishing the prisoners. I scurried to a stop when once again I felt a crack in the smooth stone.

"I feel it!" I whispered to Oscar, who was behind me.

"Okay... let's... let's drop the... the Mûrirlaplaie in 3...2...1..."

"Ahhhhhhh!" I heard someone below us scream. But it wasn't my parents or the prisoner's screams, they were Oscar's. And I had dropped my thirty Mûrirlaplaie with him.

"Oscar!" I screeched his name as a ball of fire flew up in the air, catching my hair on fire, and making the maze crumple and fall over, as if it were a set of dominos, flinging me in the ashy and smoky air. The fall was almost like it was in slow motion. I could feel the individual ashes as the air grew thicker and thicker, making it hard for me to breath. The hot ground burned me when I touched it, leaving a burn on my nose.

I shook my hair, but I only burned my hands. "Oscar! Oscar!" I called out, but I could only hear the screams of the children that were being eaten alive by the fire. Regretting my decision to kill the people off in our original plan, I rushed to the screams.

"Please! Help me!" a young boy said to me. Or at least I thought that he was a young boy.

I brushed my hand against his cage, for the silver was burning hot. I was looking for the door.

"Please hurry!" the boy squealed.

"Aha! I found it!" the lock daunted me as I fingered it with it, but apparently there was no way out for him. "I'm so sorry, but the cage will not unlock," I apologized as tears fell one by one, soothing the deep burn on my nose. I walked away, my arms out in front of me. I did not want to trip over any bodies. Not that there would be any, since all of the prisoners were unfortunately locked up.

"Is that her?" I heard someone ask. I turned around, only hear the breathing of someone, along with the great fires crackling around me. The captives screaming and crying wore down. I couldn't imagine the pain that they were going through then, even though I had bared the pain of a knife in my leg, losing my sister and best friend, going blind. Those were all pains, mental and physical, but the people who had died had gone through so much more than I had. They may have had smaller battles than I did, but they sure did have battles. Maybe their parents got divorced, or their cousin died. Perhaps they had been a victim of cancer, or even more.

Now this would now be the end of their own little war that they were fighting in.

```
Chapter 28- The End of Dolor
Aegritudo In Ocul Familia De La
Grene.
```

I could hear the footsteps of the person come closer, and closer to me. I waited patiently so I could possibly identify who it was even though the way my heart pounded and my palms sweat (not from the intense heat) told me to back away and run, even though I was blind.

Finally, I had to know who the mysterious person was, so I called out to them. "Who are you?" after about five seconds, as if the person had to process what to say, a scratchy voice called back, "I am your lifeblood, the person that gave birth to you, the person that fed you, the person that will continue to feed you until the very day you die. And now you may ask yourself, what day is that? The day that you will perish? That day is today."

"Mom? Where are you," I called to her.

"Right in front of you. Can't you see me? I am holding a knife on your neck preparing to slaughter you a- oof!" I kicked my mother, and searched the ground for Mûrirlaplaie. The explosion had blasted all of the gravestones away, and it singed the fruit. I found a few that were burned, and I prayed that they would work. I climbed up what was left of the rickety stone walls, clutching the bundle of Mûrirlaplaie in my mouth, and threw them down, not knowing what the result would be. A hot breeze flew up, tickling my sooty cheeks but I did not hear any explosions go off. Shoulders sagging, I layed down on the swaying wall, feeling my frail mother slowly climb up. I scooted over, letting my mother enough room to stand next to me. I could feel her setting her hand on the smooth stone, and pulling herself up. I hit and kicked my mom, trying to push her off so that she would fall to her death. But she held on, not giving in to my blows.

I heard her pull out a knife, and raise it, making it parallel to my neck. Balling up a fist, I felt the wall sway, back and forth. My heart rate sped up, and I could sense that my mother's own heart rate sped up too. There was a moment of silence so loud it made my ears ache. And then we fell. The stone bricks crushed each other, one after one. My mother and I would fall to our death. The stones would impair us, and we would break every bone in our body as the fires would roar around us.

Crash, crash, crash, we were getting closer to the ground, and at the last second I forced my mother under me, so she would cushion the great fall. I counted down in my head, 5...4...3...2...1. Ashes and dust flew up, signaling our fall.

```
                One year later-
```

"Come on, Reagan. You have to get to school," Mr. Zarccoo told me. I now lived with them, for they adopted me and Poppy. Poppy miraculously survived the fire and the maze. She escaped with the help of Oscar, who was busy bombing the area that she was in. He had stumbled upon her while bombing the maze, and only found her in her silver cage. He then used one of the Mûrirlaplaie to burst the cage door open. Like all the others, he died.

I made my way out of Dolor Aegritudo In Ocul Familia De La Grene. My mother was killed, my father died from the fire, I think. All of the maze was destroyed, and every once in awhile I would step on a dead body. It took me about another week to find my way out of the ruins, and climb out of the woods. I was sent to the hospital, where the doctors treated me with an infected stab wound, a minor eye injury, and a broken nose. (From the fall in the maze.) I had to stay there for five weeks, and Mr. and Mrs.

Zarccoo adopted me when they found out how I had been there when Nilly was murdered.

Now, I would say that I have a decent life. For the first time in forever, I actually have parents who love me, I have a guide dog who I call Yoda. Poppy is actually happy for once, and I go to a school for the blind in Kansas City, which we moved too after I told them Nilly died. And not to mention, I have friends. Two of them, to be exact and both of them are blind. Their names are Sara and Abbey.

I have truly won the war.

Epilogue

Smithton Times - August 23, 2145

Ruins found underground in Riverfalls Forest

By Airton Wayer

On Monday, archaeologist Kalinia Green-Istal found ruins of what appears to be what a maze was once. She claimed that she was digging to look for gold, and fell through a hole.

"The stone is arranged in such a...a...a pattern, that it appears to… to be a… to be in a shape that looks as if it were… that if it were made for… to get lost in it," Dr. Green-Istal said to us.

"We found dozens of preserved dead bodies, which make it look like… like people in the 21st century used it."

Dr. Green-Istal also mentioned that many of the bodies were locked up in rusted silver cages.

"Bodies are now under way for many tests, so that we can see how they died, who they are related to, and… and also the era they lived… that they lived in."

She went on to describe what the maze looked like. "There were rubbles of stone, with moss growing on them. A tattered musty brown curtain...a brown curtain would greet you. If you looked closely… at the… at the overgrown grass, you see the faint outline of...of little gravestones. The sky, it's...it's almost mesmerizing. In reality, you would only see… only see dirt, and it would be… it would be dark. But this sky… it is almost like a real sky, and I predict… I predict that there is… that there is magic involved."

Scientist Geloi Simono predicts that the maze was used to kill, since there is blood spilled especially in an enclosed area labeled in Ancient English as "Slaughter Room.''

"I see signs of blood everywhere in that space and it is on the floor, splattered on the walls. It is especially disturbing since the blood seems more recent," he told us.

We will report more on the issue when the information is available.

The end.